HOME GROUND

For Alison

Crumps Barn Studio
No.2 The Waterloo, Cirencester GL7 2PZ
www.crumpsbarnstudio.co.uk

Copyright © Crumps Barn Studio 2024

The rights of Diana Alexander, Patrick Booth, Amaris Chase, Stephen Connolly, Toby Crabbe, Myles Cutler, Daphne Denley, J.J. Drover, Jenny Finch, Vicki Fletcher, Nikolina Hua, Rose Leicester, Olive Malcolm, Rebecca McDowall, Rosalind Newton, Margaret Royall, Stuart Samuel, Derek Skinner, Julie Wiltshire and Ceri Vyner to be identified as the authors of this work has been asserted by them in accordance with the Copyright, Designs and Patents Act 1988.

Cover design and illustrations by Lorna Gray. All rights reserved.

Printed in the UK by Severn, Gloucester on responsibly sourced paper

MIX
Paper | Supporting
responsible forestry
FSC® C022174

ISBN 978-1-915067-48-7

HOME GROUND

mystery and magic, short stories and poetry
in a familiar landscape

DIANA ALEXANDER   PATRICK BOOTH   AMARIS CHASE

STEPHEN CONNOLLY   TOBY CRABBE   MYLES CUTLER

DAPHNE DENLEY   J.J. DROVER   JENNY FINCH

VICKI FLETCHER   NIKOLINA HUA   ROSE LEICESTER

OLIVE MALCOLM   REBECCA MCDOWALL

ROSALIND NEWTON   MARGARET ROYALL   STUART SAMUEL

DEREK SKINNER   JULIE WILTSHIRE   CERI VYNER

Crumps Barn Studio

FOREWORD

The idea for this collection grew from a discussion with artist Alison Vickery about forming an exhibition of her paintings. Or perhaps the idea for the exhibition came from this book – it is hard to be completely sure which came first. Either way, Alison was inspired to allow me (and the public) to take a closer look at the practice of an artist who has a strong relationship with a specific landscape – and in my turn, I was inspired to reach out to authors for whom the setting is a key element in their narrative.

The result is a collection which represents an extraordinary collaboration between paint and the printed word.

HOME GROUND was launched on 27 January 2024, the opening day of the exhibition by the same name. Because setting is important here, I'll add that this book will have been unboxed in our Cirencester bookshop and gallery, in a heritage building with thick stone walls and an old wood and glass frontage. It will have been surrounded by artworks painted from life in the heart of Gloucestershire. Through the medium of gouache and watercolour on paper, Alison's artworks capture the changing light, sounds and seasons. Seen from the perspective of a curator, the thrilling part for me of her body of work is its self-expression – and the sense that no moment is ever the same as the one which has gone before.

It is the perfect match for the experience of editing the contributions for this book. Each of the authors' short stories, poems and memoir shorts led me on a voyage into their own sense of magic within a landscape they know well.

Sometimes gothic, sometimes awe-inspiring, and frequently touched with the mystery of a fairy tale, this is the known world as the creative mind sees it – familiar, honest, and gloriously full of surprises.

Lorna Brookes
Crumps Barn Studio

THE PLACE

MYLES CUTLER

I spent many years working in an office and took early retirement to become a gardener. It's a generally easy and pleasant job with lots of tea and chats, fresh air and flowers. But sometimes, I wonder if myself and other gardeners are just tinkering at the edges, that what we do has no permanence, and no real place in the world as it was intended to be and perhaps as it will be again, one day. Here is an account of one of those days of wondering.

I had been working one day a week every two weeks for a lovely old couple who owned a large house on the A38 about six miles north of Thornbury in Gloucestershire. We got on well and one day the lady of the house asked me if I would be interested in taking on an additional garden for them. I said that I would be happy to and asked what the garden was like.

"Oh similar size to this one. A little overgrown perhaps. And a little isolated."

I said that I had had a cancellation and so would be able to go round in a few days time if I could have the address. The lady asked me if I was sure and I noticed that she wasn't looking directly at me but slightly to my side at the countryside that bordered the far edge of the garden. I laughed and said that gardening was my job and that I was sure it would be fine.

She looked back at me, "I'll give you the address and write out some directions for you. I won't be there to meet you. You'll be working alone."

A few days later I was putting the address into the satnav and started out to the new garden. I had been to another customer that morning but it was late summer and there was still plenty of day time left, I thought, for a bit of preliminary maintenance.

I was bowling along when the satnav suddenly said, "turn left into Midsummer Lane."

I braked so sharply that the car behind me almost went into the back of the van. The road was tiny but the satnav displayed *Midsummer Lane* and a line going forward so I put the van into gear and continued slowly. The lane went steeply downhill then levelled out and entered a wood.

The lane was now little more than a bridleway. Grass grew up the middle and there was no real roadside. The tree canopy crowded overhead and the light that came through had a curious golden quality. Like something half-forgotten.

On the left was an old post-and-rail fence and beyond it what looked a large garden now long forgotten and left alone. The satnav announced, "Proceed to the route" and displayed the word *road* above the route line. It did this when it was lost.

I thought of stopping to take a picture of the view

through the windscreen to send to friends with a caption like "Is this really the right way?!" Something in the old garden caught my eye, and then it was gone. I had the feeling that it was neither interested nor disinterested in me, as if I was literally just passing through. I decided not to stop and was wondering if this really was the right way when the woods ended and I came to a tiny junction. The satnav recovered and said to turn left. I went past a small church. This was the landmark that the customer had told me to look out for. A hundred metres on and I found the driveway to the garden.

The garden was built around all sides of a detached cottage with a high mixed hedge of wild damson, holly, and hawthorn. The damson in the hedge was sending out runners into the borders, and holly seedlings were coming up between the slabs of an old Yorkstone patio.

Behind the cottage, stone steps led up to a very large raised area of rough grass; like a paddock or an old orchard. It was bordered by an ancient high hedge with beds of nettles and brambles at its feet, and a row of conifers growing so close together that they must have been planted as a hedge decades ago and forgotten. Now they were as high as ships masts and only green at the top. Great bare patches of missing bark marked the trunks. I wondered how they could still be alive.

I climbed out of my cab and followed the path around the cottage, past beds now over-grown with weeds, and wild seeded saplings of ash and poplar. An old wooden arbour stood at the edge of a few apple trees. Bits of its own decay lay around it, overgrown with grass.

I saw what looked like bulrushes growing out of the grass where two hedges met, forming a corner. Intrigued I made my way over and found a decent sized pond, shaped like a quarter circle and now completely overgrown. I was trying to see if there was still water in it when a blackbird hopped out the hedge and passed me. It was so old that some of its feathers were streaked with white. Without stopping it regarded me briefly as if I was of no importance, made its way to the pond, and, as dignified as it could, across the rough growth and into the bulrushes. I suddenly had the childish notion that this was the bird's house, that it was an old bird, and it deserved to be respected and left alone.

I went back down to the cottage. Yellow loosestrife and Hart's Tongue ferns grew from cracks between the stones of the path. I came to the kitchen window and glanced in. Mare's Tail was coming out from under the sink. I was shocked. It looked like a green invasion; something not meant to be there.

At the gable end of the cottage I found a large buddleja growing against the wall. It had overgrown a path so I decided to cut it back to ground level. I started cutting out the many stems and adding them to a growing pile on the lawn. I had cleared down to about head height when I saw a small iron hatch cover in the wall.

I cut the rest of the stems to the base and stepped towards the hatch. On it there was an embossed image of the Green Man. Oak leaves adorned his face and hair, fern fronds made his beard, and hawthorn berries on long stems grew from the sides of his mouth. His eyes looked directly and impassively at me. I thought of Tom Bombadil in *The Lord of the Rings:* he puts on the ring and laughs at the reactions of the Hobbits. "Did you think that I would disappear?" he says. And here is the Green Man, a force of nature, conveying the same thing.

I lifted the cover off its latch and slowly pulled it open. Nothing, just an empty iron box. I was thinking, "What could this have been used for ..." when an odd feeling made me look round. I was startled to see a large bird standing on the lawn no more than two metres from me. Was it a Raven or a Crow? I didn't know how to tell. I did know that birds turn their heads to look at things but this one didn't. It was head-on to me. The point of its beak merged into its sleek head, which merged into its folded wings and body. It was as black as pitch and absolutely still. Half uneasy and half-curious, I watched the bird while I swung the hatch closed behind me. It caught on the latch and I turned quickly to shut it properly. I turned back and the bird was gone. I looked on the grass for traces but found nothing.

I cut up the buddleja branches and stacked them under a carport that was fast becoming derelict. A small hawthorn was growing out of the base of one of the metal poles that held up the roof. I went to the van and came back with a tree lifter. I put the jaws of the tool around the trunk of the hawthorn, worked my hands back to the end of the steel bar attached to the jaws, and then pulled down on the bar. Nothing happened. I leant on the bar and pushed down. The hawthorn did not move. I put all my weight on the bar, bouncing it to try to work the roots of the hawthorn loose from the ground. Suddenly I had a vision of the jaws shattering and a large jagged piece of them flying towards my face. I quickly let go of the bar. I realised what I was doing was pointless and dangerous. It was just a hawthorn. Let it be. As I tried to free the jaws from the trunk, a thorn went through my trousers and into my thigh. I cursed loudly and wrenched the jaws free.

I wondered what to do next. There wasn't a lot of daylight left but I decided that there was enough time to cut the front hedge. I put on my visor and ear defenders and started work with my favourite long arm trimmer.

The hedge was tougher than I had thought and it was slow going. Dusk was starting to fall when I got to the last section, directly in front of the cottage. I was cutting away when I thought I heard voices. I stopped to listen. Nothing. I looked around and jumped at my own reflection in a window. "Idiot" I said to myself and started cutting again. Someone said, "Who are you?" I spun round, trimmer still running. There was no one there. I stopped the trimmer and walked to the garden gate. I looked up and down the lane. No one. I looked along the hedge and decided it would do. As I walked across the lawn back to the van there was a sound of creaking. It was the old conifers moving in the wind.

The garden and cottage were falling into darkness.

I packed the van quickly and then looked around me to make sure that I hadn't left anything. A silent shape glided just above the lawn and up into the conifers. It was an owl. I told myself that it was the owl that I had heard. Not "Who are you?" but *too-wit too-woo*. I pulled out into the lane and got out to shut the big gates behind me. The air felt damp and there was the beginning of a ground mist around the garden.

I told myself that going back through the woods would be the 'long way round' and so continued down the lane. I passed some cottages shut up against the night and then the lane ended incongruously at the edge of a modern housing estate at the edge of Thornbury. I drove for while until I got my bearings and then pulled over to ring the customer. I said that the garden was a little too big for me and that perhaps a grounds maintenance company might be more appropriate. Without thinking I blurted out, "It's a special place."

The customer said, "Yes, it is. I used to live there as a little girl, and then we had to …" she paused "… leave." She added, "Sometimes it's better to let nature take its course."

VILLANELLE

MINCHINHAMPTON
MUSHROOMS

JULIE WILTSHIRE

Round and round fairies dance with gossamer wings,
Illusional, shimmering, scintillating prancers,
Weaving magic in Minchinhampton,
    in mystical rings.

Night's phantasmal mist fondles the scene,
Sinister spores, from pores, in silence advances,
Round and round fairies dance with gossamer wings.

Milky mushrooms appear from a spidery
    webbed dream.
Peek-a-boo, necromancers, moonlight dancers,
Weaving magic in Minchinhampton,
    in mystical rings.

The wise owl hoots and the nightingale sings,
Gourmet canopies popping, are shaking
    their flounces,
Round and round fairies dance with gossamer wings.

Surreal silhouettes awaiting day's dawning,
Sew circular threads on the scene, so entrancing,
Weaving magic in Minchinhampton,
    in mystical rings.

Daisies hide in the mushrooms and sharp
    swords of green,
Unspooling their chains before daylight pounces.
Round and round fairies dance with gossamer wings,
Weaving magic in Minchinhampton,
    in mystical rings.

A NORWEGIAN FAIRYTALE

MARGARET ROYALL

G randpa Olsen called the children to come and sit by the stove.

'Why can't we go up to the deserted hamlet on the ridge, Grandpa?' said Freya.

I really want to go there!"

'You said you would tell us why not. What happened there?' said her brother Jarle.

'Pull your seats up, both of you, and I will tell you exactly why not,' the old man replied. 'Listen carefully and heed my warning. You will see why no one dares to visit anymore.'

'Many years ago there was a young Scottish couple hiking in Norway. They came to the Hardanger Fjord and heard the locals' tales of an abandoned hamlet up on the ridge, where evil spirits lurked. Warned not to go exploring there they foolishly brushed off the rumours as local superstition and thought it would be interesting to climb up and take a look for themselves. Old Jonas Hansen was living nearby at the time and this is the tale he tells about what happened that fateful day. And believe me, old Jonas is a hundred years old and never lies!'

Whooooosh! Whooooosh! An invisible hand scooped Sheena up from the death-defying slope where she lay prostrate, her glasses spattered with mud, her dignity wounded. Whooooosh! The next instant she was picking her way through sodden meadows, trying hard to avoid the puddles quickly filling up with rain. It had been raining on and off now for five days, in fact more or less the whole of their Norwegian hiking trip so far.

'Oh, there you are!' Her husband Alastair had somehow already made it further up the clearing. 'How on earth did we get here?'

'No idea, it's really weird!' Sheena shook her head in confusion and a thousand tiny rainbow droplets dripped down from her tousled curls, plopping on to her sturdy walking boots.

Glancing around they could just make out the hamlet with its collection of old barns and solid houses set around a clearing. Centrally placed they noticed a large wooden outbuilding whose high-set windows framed by striped curtains reminded Sheena of the village halls she was used to back home in the Highlands of Scotland, often the village base for local scout and guide meetings and Women's Institute events. Her mouth watered briefly at the thought of custard puffs and those amazing home-made jam and cream scones she loved. She could certainly do with a cuppa and a bite to eat now!

'Hi there! Need a place to shelter?' A sprightly old chap with a healthy complexion and upright stature called out to them. Seeing their bedraggled state he

13

beckoned them to take shelter in the hut.

'Hello, I'm Per. Pleased to meet you.' He shook their hands vigorously, a little too vigorously for Alastair's liking.

'I'm eighty six years old, I've lived here all my life,' he said.

He clearly stemmed from a generation of hardy country folk who possessed a natural understanding of the laws of nature. He was dressed in khaki cargo pants and bottle green jumper, with a paisley neckerchief tied neatly round his neck secured by a wooden toggle. He reminded Sheena of an overgrown Boy Scout. She half expected him to suddenly shout 'Dib dib, dob dob.'

In other circumstances the couple might have made their polite excuses and beaten a hasty retreat, since they were immediately spooked by this chap's appearance, but given the appalling weather and the state of their sodden raincoats and mud-caked boots they figured that a brief spell sheltering in the hut was bearable. After all, what could possibly happen to them up here in this mountain hideaway?

Once inside they had a chance to check out their surroundings.

'What's that scary thing over there?' Alastair's pointed to the far end of the room.

'There on the wall you mean? Ah yes, that's our old Norwegian bull, Odin. Strong character he was too, a warmonger, just like his namesake! Feared by all creatures, unchallenged in his lifetime.'

Per pointed to the huge brindle hide fastened across the rear wall. At Per's invitation they stroked the pelt, marvelling at the bristly texture of the hairs which prickled their palms as they caressed it. Sheena, who loved working with textiles, was particularly fascinated by the feel of it and stroking the pelt lulled her into an almost trance-like state.

'Beware the God of War!' Per's thundering voice boomed out, startling them. The whole demeanour of this previously affable villager had transformed in a flash. His eyes narrowed to thin slits, his lips were pursed and taut and he seemed to be leering at them in a weird manner.

Sheena and Alastair were caught off guard by this strange turn of events and with a quick glance at each other decided it was time to leave. With a hasty thanks and goodbye they headed for the exit and didn't dare to look back. Alastair grabbed Sheena by the arm and pulled her towards the downhill path, now waterlogged and barely discernible.

'Weird guy, don't you think? Gave me the creeps!' he said, zipping his anorak up to his nose. He seized Sheena's hand and yanked her back towards the path.

'I don't fancy climbing back down those lethal steps. It's like scaling a waterfall,' said Sheena. Her face was pale and anxious and she shook at the thought of the downward climb. 'This place feels like it's been possessed by evil spirits. Goodness knows what might happen to us!' Her anxiety was palpable.

Alastair, clearly irritated by his wife's fanciful thoughts, tutted loudly. 'Just leave off with all your parapsychology, will you! The guy is clearly deranged. The sooner we start the sooner we'll get back down to the car. This rain is set in for the day, no use waiting.'

No sooner had they accomplished the first leg of the descent than things took an even weirder turn. From the scowling heavens the rain lashed mercilessly down. They shook with cold and their lips took on a bluish tinge. The supposedly waterproof jackets were no longer up to the job and the oozing mud clinging tenaciously to their boots impeded their progress.

'Look, there's a rough shelter over there. Let's keep dry inside until this storm eases,' said Alastair, pointing to a shack off to their right. Sheena needed no encouragement. She was already scrambling up the slope, clawing at the muddy stones to gain a foothold. Once inside they found a pile of old sacks from which they fashioned a makeshift seat. Huddled exhausted together their eyes became droopy and they drifted into an uneasy slumber.

Whooooosh! Whooooosh! An uncanny sound coming from the roof space overhead jolted them back to reality. They became aware of an angry presence accompanied by a putrid stench. This was the stuff of horror movies. In mad panic they decided on flight rather than fight, but their limbs were glued to the spot. Then, just as they contemplated the prospect of imminent death, there it came again – *Whooooosh! Whooooosh!* As suddenly as it had come the evil spirit was gone and they were back in their bodies, wiggling toes and fingers and trying to stand on stiff legs. As though a raging lion were on their tail they bolted down the steps, twisting, turning and finally toppling headlong into the path of a local walking his dog. At first they failed to recognise him. He gesticulated wildly up at the haunted shelter, his eyes dark and threatening.

'Aha, so you dared to enter Odin's inner sanctum, did you, and brought his vengeance upon yourselves?'

There was an alien ring to the man's words, but on further scrutiny his features morphed seamlessly into those of Per. Then, a second later, he vanished.

With indecent haste the spooked couple raced on down the track and flung themselves into their car. Alastair turned the ignition key and the vehicle shot out onto the road by the fjord, windscreen wipers whizzing back and forth.

Sheena could hardly catch her breath, her words jamming in her throat. 'W-w-w-what j-just h-h-happened th-there?'

'No idea, but don't let's wait to find out!' Alastair gritted his teeth and clung to the steering-wheel for dear life.

The car turned off down a side road, heading for their B&B on a remote farm. Gradually they began to relax a little, feeling the tension leave their bodies.

Whooooosh! Whooooosh! With no warning an invisible

hand descended from the heavens and scooped up the car and its passengers. For a few seconds a message formed from blobs of leaking oil was visible on the road – *ODIN IS AVENGED*, it read – *BEWARE THE WRATH OF ODIN*. Then, almost instantly, it was gone!

Grandpa Olsen sat back in his chair. 'So, children, that is why you are forbidden to ever go up to the hamlet,' he said sternly. 'For make no mistake, you might never come back again!' Freya and Jarle, silenced by the tale, nodded at him, vowing never ever to visit the haunted hamlet. Indeed they kept their promise. But in years to come they could be found sitting by the stove with their own grandchildren, relating the same spooky tale.

LOST IN ACTION

DEREK SKINNER

One of the advantages, if there are any, of 'getting on a bit', is that family and friends tend to offer you lifts, rather than running the risk of trusting your driving. Due to a slight deafness, I'd given up trying to follow the animated family conversation going on in the front seat. I'd been staring absentmindedly out of the car window at the passing scenery, when with a sudden shock, everything came sharply into focus. I knew exactly where I was. I hadn't realized we would be going this way. In an instant, I was transported back nearly eighty years. I looked across the road. Yes, there was the bus stop. I was a small boy, waiting at that very bus stop for the 156 bus that would take me to my school in Sutton, no school buses in those days.

It was the sight of the George Inn that had triggered it all. It was almost the George Inn of old, now with a few modern flourishes and painted and tarted up a bit, but quite unmistakably the building imprinted in my memory. On that day, very nearly eighty years ago, I'd had a close brush with death.

"Stop!" I shrilled. Startled, my daughter who was doing the driving, drew in and I explained. We all got out and walked back up to the bus stop where it had all happened. It was a day, remarkably like today, bright with early summer sunshine and an azure clear sky.

I had been standing at that bus stop in my red school blazer and smart red cap. I remember rather dreading going to school that day and also feeling very guilty. I usually shared my worries with my mother who somehow always understood and would set my mind at rest. I couldn't this time because I had told her a lie. I'd said we hadn't been set a prep, so that I could go out and play with the gang in the now lengthening summer evenings. Now I would have to think of some excuse as to why I had not done my prep.

Mr Cassidy, old 'Hopalong' – he'd lost a leg in the First World War but was actually nicknamed after the American Cowboy hero Hopalong Cassidy, and was thus doubly qualified for the name – took no prisoners. I might be kept in at the end of school and that would mean more lies to my mum. Life was unfair.

Then I heard a noise, one that I had heard only once before. I knew instantly what it was. I knew also that somehow it might offer salvation to a mind grasping at straws.

What I heard was the growly rumbling approach of a Doodlebug, the German's first flying bomb. It was Hitler's terror weapon, but how could you possibly be frightened of something as friendly sounding as a Doodlebug. How clever too of someone to give it that name. I'd seen films of the Doodlebug on the Saturday morning flicks. The Pathé News had shown footage of Spitfires flying well above the height of the approaching Doodlebug and then screaming down in a power dive with throttles full out. It was the only way they could match the speed of the rocket powered German aircraft. The Spit would rake it with its twenty-millimeter cannon until it burst into flame and spiraled down, hopefully into open farmland. Another more daring method on the newsreel was for the Spit to fly briefly alongside the Doodlebug and to edge its wing tip under the rocket's stubby little wings. Then the Spitfire would roll sharply over, throwing the doodlebug into a spin with all its guidance gyros going haywire. It would dive harmlessly into farmland below. This was stuff us schoolboys all knew off by hat.

Now my eyes scanned the clear blue of the sky to see if I could actually catch sight of the approaching rocket. Then I saw it. It was flying much lower than their bombers flew. Only as it neared, could you appreciate the speed it was going. The sound of its grumbling rumbling approach increased. Then, in a moment the little craft seemed to stagger in the sky. A second later the sound reached me of the engine's stutter. Abruptly, it ceased altogether. The sudden silence seemed unnatural. The Doodlebug began a slow arching fall towards where I stood.

My first thoughts were, *Wow! Wait till I get back to school. No one had ever yet watched a real Doodlebug, let alone seen one actually coming down.* Only then did it occur to me that I might be in some sort of danger.

I dived to the ground, but I had to look up. I wasn't going to miss a moment of this. It was so much bigger than I had imagined. I could see its sleek shark shape with the rocket motor perched on its tail. The whistling sound of its descent grew shriller and more urgent. 'If you can hear it whistling, it's got your name on it', was the adage about ordinary bombs. Did that apply also to doodlebugs I wondered? It was coming straight to where I was lying. At the very last moment, I shut my eyes.

The ground heaved up under me. There was a tremendous explosion. The air seemed to be sucked out of my lungs. I was conscious of being picked up and bowled over and over like a rag doll. The ground shook as great boulders of masonry thudded to earth about me. Then an eerie silence. All I could hear was a constant whistling in my eardrums. Everything seemed to have stopped. Everything was still. Slowly I opened my eyes which I realized then were still tightly closed. The whole world had changed.

I found myself somehow in the middle of the road. My first instinct was to get back off the road in case I got run over, though it would have taken a bulldozer to have fought through the piles of rubble about me. I slowly took stock. Apart from a few grazes I was unharmed. The bomb had exploded in the garden of The George inn. The George was still standing, but somehow stripped naked. The bones of the roof were exposed, not a tile remained in place. Every window was shattered, the blackout curtains all shredded and fluttering in the wind. The air was full of the familiar aroma of smoke and the tang of high explosives. But what struck me most of all was that it had suddenly changed in a flash from summer to mid-winter, for not a leaf remained on any of the trees. They too had been stripped naked.

My mother, in a panic quickly arrived on the scene and hugged me as I'd never been hugged before, muttering something over and over again. But I couldn't hear what she was saying for the whistling in my ears. I was taken home and pampered as I'd never been pampered before.

More than anything though I was relieved. Relieved that now I would not have to face the withering interrogation from old Hopalong. I couldn't wait to get back to school, to tell all the others about me and the Doodlebug. I also rehearsed my conversation with Hopalong. "Frightfully sorry 'bout your Prep Sir. Did enjoy doin' the sums and that. 'Fraid my exercise book got total blown up by one of Hitler's Doodlebug things Sir. Tried to save it Sir. It got sort of lost in action Sir."

UNSETTLED

ROSALIND NEWTON

When I look back at the week spent in the cottage in Northumberland, my home county, I remain mystified by what occurred there, but it altered my life.

It had been an exhausting year with Max – I was uncertain about our relationship. I was very tired and desperate for some time to myself in order to relax and get my thoughts in order. The cottage rental had been my sister's idea. Harriet was always full of good ideas.

Our parents had owned a holiday cottage on the moors near Rothbury but it had to be sold when Dad's firm was in financial difficulties. Harriet trawled the internet and found a small cottage with one bedroom to rent and it wasn't too far from the cottage we remembered from childhood holidays.

So I leapt at the chance of leaving the city and driving to Northumberland for a week's stay in the little cottage called Chirm Well. I recollect looking up the word "chirm" to find it meant, rather charmingly, a flock of finches. The cottage was surrounded by ivy-engulfed trees, and had been modernised so I realised it would be more comfortable than the cottage of my childhood. Autumn was fast approaching, and I was cold so the first thing I did on arrival was light the log fire in the small sitting room. It had a dining table with chairs and a rocking chair plus some books in a small bookcase.

After supper I decided to take a walk down the lane. The night scents of leaf sap and bracken filled my lungs. Ahead of me lay a pool, darkly gleaming like tarnished silver. By the light of the moon I could see a shape and heard a voice, rather high-pitched. The note changed and became like a dirge!

I turned and fled, being overtaken by sheer, blinding panic, and stumbled back along the track. I was stung by nettles and then ran from the wood back to the cottage. It was a relief to return to the warm cottage. On going to bed I fell eventually into a dreamless sleep. This little break had not so far been at all relaxing and I was unsettled and anxious and decided not to take another evening walk during my stay.

The next few days were uneventful and I relaxed at last, finding walks on the moors exhilarating enough to erase memories of that awful night-time walk at the beginning of my stay.

I drove to the nearby market town of Rothbury and enjoyed a lunch at a country inn. One day when it was warmer I even enjoyed a picnic on the wonderful moors surrounding my temporary home.

Nearing the end of my break away I returned to the cottage in the late afternoon with more provisions, looking forward to catching up later on some reading which I had always enjoyed but lately had neglected – my mind being full of thoughts about Max and what had become a fraught relationship. My job was beginning to suffer as my concentration was poor. But one of my pleasures on that little holiday was pottering in the small kitchen and that particular evening I made a favourite pasta dish to enjoy with a glass of white wine. After the meal I washed up in the kitchen and returned to the sitting room planning to read my novel in front of the log fire.

I put my hand to my mouth in total shock to find an old woman in the rocking chair.

I had heard no one ring the doorbell of the cottage whilst in the kitchen. My heart began to pound. Something weird was happening again to me on this supposed break away from the chaos of my normal life. My thoughts were very jumbled: shock, horror and a mixture of anger and despair. How dare this old woman come into this cottage! It scared me to see how comfortable this intruder seemed to be as she gently rocked in the chair. I noticed her very lined face and penetrating blue-grey eyes, her white hair was tied up I supposed into a bun. I was surprised to see she was wearing a long cotton skirt and blouse which was unsuitable attire for the autumn chill.

"How dare you come in here!" I managed to exclaim. I was certain I had locked the door.

The woman had a rich Northumbrian burr when she replied with a slow smile. "I let myself in as I lived here when I was a young woman."

"I don't believe you," I replied firmly, "I'm very security-conscious and would never leave the front door open!"

In response my uninvited guest once again just gave that slow smile, which infuriated me.

"You don't have the right to come in here to invade my privacy and give me a shock. I want you to leave right now! I've had one awful experience already this week and don't need another!' I shrieked.

This supposed holiday was becoming a joke. The woman seemed to be oblivious to my outburst and quietly responded with an annoying calmness.

"I suppose you must have heard me by the pool one evening. I find myself returning there you see …" Her face crumpled somewhat and she continued to rock in the chair whilst I glared at her.

She ignored my pleas for her to leave and was audacious enough to ask me quite firmly to sit down and hear her out. To my astonishment and despite misgivings I found myself doing just that.

The old woman went on, "I go there quite often when it's dark – just like it was when it happened … I still miss him and it would be me you heard wailing." She paused as if to catch breath. "You're young and pretty and I assume you have a gentleman in your life."

The old woman went on to tell me that she had romantic trysts by the pool with a young man called Arthur whom she loved. They planned to elope one day. The pool became their meeting place at dusk. Her voice became soft as she recalled that her lover had slipped and fallen into the pool. It was much deeper than anticipated. "He fell into the pool and was sucked under the water as he stumbled. I was rooted to the spot as I could not swim and Arthur was too far out. It all happened so fast and I watched him sinking, then sinking some more … there were bubbles when Arthur's head disappeared. The bubbles stopped, and I couldn't reach him!"

She covered her eyes with bony hands. I was listening to this old person recounting this awful story and suddenly my anger began to evaporate. Haltingly she continued to talk to me. "All I can say to you my dear is to seize the day while you can and don't wait too long to get together if you love someone, as I believe you do," she paused again as I listened intently. "You see we all have faults. Arthur and I had all those plans and yet we were scared to elope as we knew our families would not be able to forgive us. It was different all those years ago. We argued a lot about our future together but he was the love of my life."

I remember feeling sudden compassion for this elderly intruder who had earlier invaded my space. What the old lady was wearing was far too flimsy for a chill evening and I recall offering to make her a cup of tea. The old woman accepted, saying, "You're kind. Please remember my advice to seize the day – find love whilst you can and don't be alone like me wishing things were different."

Once again her gaze was penetrating. Wordlessly I rose and went to the kitchen, gulping down a glass of water whilst the kettle boiled. I returned with the mug in my hand to the sitting room to find it was empty. My visitor had gone! The rocking chair was still rocking so perhaps I had not imagined the encounter, but the old lady had disappeared as silently as she had arrived. I had not heard the door shut. I opened it and looked outside but there was no one about. The wind had risen, and I felt very alone.

The encounter mystified me. Was my imagination playing tricks? Was I hallucinating? The old lady was urging me to seize the day. I stared into the fire and thought of Max. What was he doing just now? I had blamed Max far too many times and had overlooked his strengths whilst concentrating on his weaknesses and totally ignoring my own. Suddenly I reached for my mobile phone.

DARK MAGIC

OLIVE MALCOLM

The last ghostly
skeletons of leaves
haunt the forest floor
with the death rattle
of decay
shape-shifting shadows
blur the boundary between
the living and the dead.

Naked trees
raise twisted limbs
to a bloodstained sky
like a coven of witches
chanting
secret incantations
to the hunter's moon
a shiver of magic
thrills the night.

Mischief is afoot
pumpkin lanterns leer
as ghosts and ghouls
plague the living
a black-clad familiar
stalks the streets
on silent
velvet pads.

A crackling starburst
stabs the sky
the stench of sulphur
chokes dry throats
as flames lick
the traitor
tortured screams
of a Catherine wheel
rip the smoke-laden air.

Cross her palm with silver
Madame Sosostris
clairvoyant
veiled in shadow
deals the tarot
spins the wheel of fortune
discerns the future
in the heavenly constellations
of the stars.

THE ENCHANTED FIELD

DIANA ALEXANDER

Midsummer Day. My birthday. A perfect summer morning, the children were at school, and I was going riding on my pony, Rocket.

Riding was one of the things I liked doing most in the world. It was fun to go out with my children but even better, just occasionally, was to go on my own, think my own thoughts and enjoy the magnificent scenery which was almost on my doorstep.

Misarden Park was a wonderland of woods, fields, streams and lakes with tracks which connected them all and it was just one field away from where I lived. The generous landowner allowed us free access to the park as long as we didn't venture into the very few 'no go' areas – and we never did.

Rocket jig-jogged along, glad to be out on this lovely day and, as always, with adventure on his mind. We crossed the lane outside our house and then the field which led into the wood. We went down a steep track and followed the stream which flowed through the park. Wild orchids grew by the track and I caught a glimpse of bright blue and knew that the wild gentians were just coming into bloom.

In what seemed a very short time, the track ended and we went through a narrow gate into a field that, unusually, I didn't recognise. Rocket stopped jogging and walked along, ears pricked, clearly intrigued by this strange and beautiful place.

For beautiful it certainly was. The whole meadow was a mass of wild flowers and grasses. Pink campion mingled with blue cranesbill and lacy meadowsweet whose scent filled the air. There were dog daisies and wild purple scabious and many grasses to which I couldn't put a name. Butterflies of every size and colour fluttered in the ever-warming air – among them peacocks and red admirals and I thought I even saw a flash of colour which just could have been the large blue butterfly, rare at that time. I felt that anything could happen on that magical day.

The birdsong was extraordinary – every bird for miles seemed to be singing its own particular song. Not for the first time, I wished I was better at recognising each one. But even I could identify the cuckoo, now seldom heard, who was a regular summer visitor in those days. Swallows swooped to and fro and way overhead a skylark hovered, singing his little heart out.

In what seemed like a few minutes but which turned out to be nearly an hour, we arrived back at the gate where we had first gone in. That was unusual – most fields in the park had a gate at either end, leading on to another track.

"We'll go there another day," I said, partly to Rocket, partly to myself, as he jogged merrily home, released from the spell.

Try as I might, I never found that field again.

RIDE OF THE POOKA

PATRICK BOOTH

Ireland is magic. You can close your eyes and just know you're there. The sound of the birds, the rustle of the trees, even the silence is imbued with an emotion that you do not feel when you're anywhere else. A small island on the edge of a huge ocean, the westernmost frontier of the old world that always retained a sense of mystery and ethereal otherworldliness.

Michael fondly remembered the summer holidays he spent there as a child at his grandparents' farm on the Beara Peninsula in the west of Cork. While his friends went to Spain, American theme parks or on cruises he felt he was luckier than all of them when he got to play in fields overlooking Bantry Bay with his cousins, walk up the nearby mountains, ride his uncle's horses or sit in a tractor being driven by his grandfather.

He had grown up listening to Irish fairy tales and heard many stories about mischievous and cunning leprechauns and knew to be wary of the banshee's cry but it was tales about the pooka that stirred his imagination the most. The pooka was a type of fairy who could take many forms both human or animal. The first time he heard the name he thought it sounded funny but his grandfather warned him the pooka could be friendly or threatening. A friendly pooka might clean the house or plough the fields for you but an unfriendly one could deceive you or take you for a wild ride upon its back.

One morning when he was 10, Michael asked his grandad about the pooka while they were counting cows in one of the fields. "Have you ever seen a pooka grandad?"

His grandad breathed in grandly as though he was about to sing at an opera. "Have I ever seen a pooka?"

Michael waited expectantly.

"I tell you truthfully Michael that I have never seen a pooka."

Michael felt his body slump in disappointment. "Do you know anybody who has seen a pooka?"

"A few of the old folks who lived round here when I was growing up say they saw one, but I don't think anybody round here has seen one for a long time."

"What did they say it looked like?"

"Well I've told you that a pooka can look like different animals. Sometimes a cow, sometimes a horse, sometimes a dog or a goat."

"What would happen if it took you for a ride on its back?"

"It would be a terrifying ride. So fast and terrible that you could barely hold on as you flew through the air."

"Could the ride kill people?"

"Yes, but it would take many wild rides before the person died. They would get weaker and weaker but they'd never be able to say no once they were under its spell."

"Did nobody survive?"

"Well it's said that one smart fella got a blacksmith to make him some special spurs which he wore when he went for a ride and they hurt the pooka so much it refused to ever take him again."

Michael thought about this for a while. "The ride sounds fun, like a roller coaster."

His grandfather laughed "Not everybody likes a roller coaster and the pooka doesn't come with a safety bar."

After they finished counting the cows they got back into his grandfather's car and headed back to the farmhouse. Michael spent the afternoon playing football with his cousins and other children from the local area.

That night Michael woke up. He wasn't sure why he was suddenly awake. He listened but there were no sounds in the rest of the farmhouse. He looked towards the bedroom window. Moonlight was coming through the gaps at the edges of the curtains. For some reason he felt there was something outside so he got out of bed. He went to the window, pulled the curtains apart slightly and looked outside.

The window overlooked the empty field to the rear of the farmhouse. The moon allowed him to see the outline of the mountains in the distance but then he noticed something else moving in the field.

He strained to see what it was and at first he wasn't sure if he was imagining things but then he was sure there was a black mass that seemed to be darker than everything surrounding it. It appeared to be getting closer to the stone wall surrounding the field but then it stopped and two yellow lights suddenly appeared on either side of the mass. They looked like eyes and in a split second Michael dashed back into his bed. He pulled the covers over him and turned his body so that he wasn't facing towards the window. He feared whatever it was he had seen would try and get into the farmhouse and he expected to hear the sounds of a window smashing or a door opening but the house remained silent. Eventually his breathing slowed but he could not fall back to sleep.

"Michael." The voice he heard was quiet and whispered but it seemed to echo around him. He pulled the covers back from his head and looked around but nobody was there. "Michael." He heard the voice again. He realised that he wasn't afraid. He got out of bed and slowly walked back to the window. He peeped through the gap between the curtains and the thing was still there. It seemed to be standing behind the stone wall but the glow from the yellow eyes made it difficult to make out exactly what it looked like. They looked at each other for a while and then Michael heard the voice again, "Come ride with me Michael."

Michael stepped back and the gap between the curtains closed.

He found it difficult to believe what he was seeing and hearing. Was this really a pooka? Was he dreaming? If it was a dream, it was the most realistic dream he'd ever had. Was the pooka trying to lure him to his death?

He didn't feel like he was being forced to go out and he could've gone back to bed if he wanted but he was thinking about what the ride would be like. It could be better than any roller coaster he'd ever been on but it could also be scarier than anything he'd done before. He thought about it for a few minutes and then he had an idea.

He carefully crept slowly downstairs making sure not to wake anybody in the house. He went to the back door and unlocked it. He looked down to the side of the door and saw what he was looking for, the football boots he'd been wearing that afternoon. He put them on, opened the door took a deep breath and walked outside.

His football boots made a loud clopping sound as he walked and he worried it would wake somebody up. The pooka, Michael had now decided that was definitely what he was looking at, was still standing motionless behind the stone wall. The brightness of the yellow eyes made it difficult to see exactly what the rest of it looked like. After looking at each other silently the pooka turned slowly to its left and walked to a gap in the stone wall where a gate had once been. It moved the same way a horse moved and as it came through the gap in the wall, a security light on the side of the farmhouse came on and Michael saw that it did look like a horse, jet black with bright yellow eyes. It walked on four legs but as it came closer it slowly reared up and walked just on its back legs and Michael could see that what he thought were its front feet were black hands with long wrinkly fingers ending in claws. It came closer and towered over Michael. It snorted which made Michael jump. It then crouched down in front of him and Michael looked into its yellow eyes for what felt like hours. The pooka then turned to its right and lay down and looked directly ahead. Michael knew this was his chance to mount it. He held out a trembling hand to touch the pooka's fur. It felt just like a normal horse. He took another deep breath, jumped onto its back, flung his leg over to its other side and then held tightly onto the pooka's shaggy black mane.

For a while nothing happened and then the pooka stood up, turned back towards the gap in the wall and walked through it. The walk became a trot, the trot became a gallop and they were charging across the field. Michael closed his eyes and then he felt a strange feeling in his stomach. He held on tighter and then slowly opened his eyes to see the ground below quickly fall away. They were flying. He looked ahead and the moonlight allowed him to see they were flying over the mountains. Higher they went and Michael felt cold and wet as they passed through a cloud. He could see the stars and moon above him and below him he could see the outline of the coastline marked out by the moonlight reflecting on the sea.

Suddenly the pooka turned to its right and went into a fast downward dive and Michael screamed as the ground rushed up towards them. At the last moment the pooka pulled up and they seemed to skim above the trees of a dense forest. Michael could feel his blood pumping. The ride was better than any roller coaster he had ever been on but it was also the most terrified he'd ever been. Suddenly he remembered the boots and he dug the studs into the pooka's side. It neighed angrily and it seemed to slow slightly. Michael was glad that the boots were working like the spurs his grandfather had told him about.

They whooshed through woods, over hills and from time to time he saw the lights of villages twinkling below them. At one point they passed over a city. He wondered if anybody could see them. Sometimes they went above clouds and sometimes they skimmed above the waves of the sea as vast cliffs loomed over them. From time to time Michael dug his boots into the pooka's side and the creature seemed to react by tossing its head angrily from side to side.

He was not sure how long he spent on the pooka's back during that exhilarating journey but as the first signs of light started to appear on the horizon they began to slow and descend. He wondered where they were but then he could hear the pooka's feet galloping on the ground and he realised they'd landed and as they slowed and stopped he could see they were back in the field behind the farmhouse. Michael dismounted and as he landed he collapsed onto the ground as his legs were trembling too much to be able to support his weight. The pooka looked down at him and then turned and padded away into the darkness and Michael was left alone on the ground trying to get his breath back. After a few minutes he was able to stand up and he hurried back to the house. He left his football boots by the back door and went back up to bed.

The next morning he was shaken awake by his mother. "Michael, it's midday. You've overslept. You've never done that before." He suddenly remembered the ride from the night before but he decided to not tell anybody, not even his grandfather in case it had been a dream. The next night he tried to stay awake in case the pooka came back and a couple of times he got up and looked out of the window but there was nothing there. Eventually he fell asleep. A few days later he went home to England and despite returning to Ireland many times for many years, Michael never saw the pooka again.

TOM LONG'S POST

DAPHNE DENLEY

On Minch Common's road, you'll see
    Tom Long's Post
Near the crossroads of confusion, to and
    from a through road
Ignore or give way to the cars edging out
Daren't look at the faces of drivers, they scowl
Then feel the guilt, whilst some remain stuck
You're needing to hurry, 'cus traffic's held you up
Admire the power of this simple sign
A six ways direction, that challenges minds
Willpower, drive forwards and ignore the others?
Or take your time, give way, avoiding a fluster?
Each morning, approach chaos, in traffic lines
Of dancing vehicles, trying not to collide
Landmark named after the Highwayman Tom
Criminal hung, died or buried on this spot
Alice and Wonderland sign, I kid you not
Historical junction, where traffic just stops
Has Tom had the last laugh, as trouble it is?
But this common land's beautiful
    and his legend still lives

WOODCHESTER

DAPHNE DENLEY

Dared to walk through on a darkened eve
As so much history and folklore is believed
Banshee screams, from lady of the lake?
You could disappear without a trace
Graveyard spooky, Dr Who was once filmed
Roman paving below, protected, entombed
Mansion never finished, as works gave up
Gargoyles a glaring, edge the roofs above
Playground for the dead, been filmed on TV
Venue for 'Most Haunted' at Halloween
Woodlands, lakes and fields surround
Trees roar in the wind aloft a misty shroud
Did once brave knights sit at table round?
King Arthur's legend, is Camelot found?
Aura undeniable, in the mysterious air
Spells from past and present must beware
If curious visit, more to learn and uncover
Secrets are plenty in ancient Woodchester

LIGHT & SHADOW

AMARIS CHASE

It was early one morning when the dusky pink dawn sky met the pale pink of the cherry blossom, a fox cub looking inquisitively at the pink petals silently falling around him like pink snow, that inspiration first struck Ayza. She studied this magical scene from her kitchen window: the cub had a story to tell, the tranquil, oasis of green that her flat overlooked had a story to tell, and she would tell that story through a quartet of paintings. She would depict the view from her kitchen window through each season.

She immediately grabbed a sketchbook and pencil and started doing a preliminary sketch of the cub and tree, she knew the cub wouldn't stay there long. This was the peaceful moment in the park when the birds graced the morning with their hours and before the park was occupied by people and dogs.

Ayza's ground floor flat was towards the end of a cul de sac which formed the flat edge of a crescent garden, just a small park with a variety of trees and wildflowers with some benches, a quiet haven for locals wanting to escape the chaos of the city.

Ayza's kitchen stood a couple of feet away from the park and was separated by black railings. Grey squirrels used the railing as a watch post to observe the garden.

She was able to get a good view of city wildlife from here. The railings were lined with nettles and wildflowers beside a path which coursed an arc towards the central exit from the park. There was just one wooden bench which faced the flats at an angle, so Ayza didn't feel like anyone was staring directly at her. Closer to her window was the cherry blossom tree to the left, and another mature tree to her right. Further back were younger trees and the railings of the crescent. On the other side of the park were grand Georgian town houses.

SPRING

Ayza sketched out her composition on a canvas at a small table by her kitchen window where there was a lot of light. She would make the bench the focal point of the scene.

She began work with her oil paints, capturing the pink dawn, the cherry blossom in its prime, droves of daffodils and bluebells along the perimeter of the park, the bench lying empty and silent in between. She mixed a few autumnal shades and with the simplest of strokes caught the suggestion of the fox cub watching specks of pink around him.

She captured the other trees in her view, then the part that she loved the best – which was to paint the shadows. Shadows were what made a painting, they could lift a flat and emotionless scene into something three dimensional and full of character. Shadows were what gave a painting life.

Ayza left the painting to dry overnight. She wanted to look upon the painting with fresh eyes in the morning light to check for any alterations required.

The next morning though, when she went to make her ritual coffee, she noticed a shadow painted in front of the bench, as if someone was sitting on the bench but the bench itself remained empty. It was as if there was a shadow of a ghost. She checked her preliminary sketches, and she hadn't captured any such shadow in any of them. Perhaps she had accidentally left a smudge there when painting in the shadows? She decided to paint over it and not dwell on the matter.

SUMMER

As spring segued into summer, the park became darker with the canopy of trees in full leaf, offering respite from the heat. Ayza again made preliminary sketches and then began painting a typical lunchtime scene in the park. She carefully painted a woman at the bench, eating a sandwich whilst scrolling on her phone; a small dog leapt against a tree to chase a squirrel, with its owner looking on impassively from the path. A few strokes of browns and greys indicated a squirrel further up the tree, successfully avoiding the dog.

The shadows were more dappled in the midday sun, but Ayza was proud at how she had captured the sense of heat of the day, the playfulness of the animals and the nonchalant humans.

This time when she examined the painting the next

morning, there was a shadow next to the woman on the bench, following the curved contour of the bench as if it was an imprint of someone sitting there. She was sure she hadn't painted this shadow in, she would have noticed for sure last night and she lived alone so there was no chance of anyone else tampering with the painting. Intrigue had turned to unease, Ayza needed to get out of the flat.

Later that day she met her sisters for their weekly café catch up.

"Perhaps you had a 'waking dream', suggested Mahida, the eldest of the sisters and the most level-headed.

"A waking dream? What do you mean?" Asked Ayza.

"It's when you fall asleep momentarily when you are doing an activity when awake, and you wake up thinking you had a vision, when it was just a dream. It only lasts a few seconds," explained Mahida.

"But I'm sure I didn't paint in those shadows, I checked the painting at night before going to bed!" Ayza protested.

"You paint for hours on end, Ayza, and you become so absorbed in your work that you forget to eat and rest. Your eyes must have been tired, you must have missed the shadows," Mahida said gently.

"Or you might just be going crazy going with the paints …" Bushra proffered. Mahida and Ayza looked at her puzzled. Bushra continued, "I saw this horror movie once where an artist moves house and the artist's paintings became dark and demonic and he begins to think he's being possessed by a demon. It turned out that in fact the toxic chemicals in the paint were affecting the artist's sanity."

Bushra sensed Ayza had not taken this suggestion too kindly. She waited apprehensively to be chastised as Ayza stared at Bushra with eyes blazing, but instead Ayza said in a measured tone, "I think I'll stick to the waking dream theory."

AUTUMN

Orange and gold leaves pirouetted in the air as the wind stripped trees of their leaves. This was Ayza's favourite season, she loved the autumn colour palette, the berries replacing the flowers of summer, the squirrels scurrying around with nuts in their mouth and burying them in places they invariably forgot the location of in winter. The path had become a squelching ochre mess from the decaying leaves.

Ayza again sketched scenes of the park, and this time she selected a toddler girl in her bright waterproof raincoat and wellies walking animatedly along the straight stretch of the path with her mother whose face was obscured by a hat and scarf, the little girl laughing and pointing to something outside the composition of the painting.

As much as Ayza loved autumn, there was also a sadness to it with the vibrancy and colour of summer being replaced by a more limited palette. She reflected this by painting in a figure of one of the numerous men she would see at the bench, alone with just a bottle for company. The brightness of the toddler tempered by the sadness of the man in the background. The shadows had become longer with the change of season, and Ayza was slightly nervous of what the next morning would bring to her painting. Not to be outdone, she took a photo of the painting this time before leaving it for the night. And yet, there it was in the morning, a shadow that she knew for sure now she hadn't painted as she had photographic evidence! The shadow again sat next to the man on the bench but this time the silhouette had more form, and its curves suggested a female figure with its head turned to face Ayza's flat. Ayza felt a creeping sensation run up her spine and moved the canvas to the spare room where it would be out of sight.

Later that week, over a comforting pumpkin spiced latte piled high with cream, she told her sisters of this latest development.

"That is spooky," acknowledge Mahida, "But maybe you just sleepwalked and painted it in."

"I've never sleepwalked in my life!" Ayza countered, fed up with the rational theories.

"But you may have started as a consequence of your artistic insecurities, you're forever worried your work isn't good enough," persisted Mahida.

"Or you might actually be possessed by a demon," offered Bushra unhelpfully. There was a tense pause, and this time everyone in the café turned around to look at them as Ayza exploded …

WINTER

Ayza was determined to get to the bottom of the mystery shadow in her last composition. The park was a mixture of bare and evergreen trees. It was also lighter with stripped branches of trees allowing the sunlight to filter through. The shadows were at their longest in this season, but Ayza wanted to paint the park at night where it was difficult to determine the outline of the trees and bench, and so the Georgian town houses became the focal point as they were illuminated by the street lamps. Bright LED dog collars would punctuate the darkness, as if the dogs were attending a festival, the blue blaze of phone screens made patterns in the air as teenagers hung out at the bench, but often it was the homeless who claimed the bench. One evening Ayza saw a woman at the bench light up a cigarette and for a brief moment her face lit up with the sulphureous light against the inky black of the night and it was reminiscent of a Rembrandt painting. This would be Ayza's composition.

Ayza mixed blues, greys and blacks for the foreground, and warmer browns and oranges for the buildings in the background. She painted late into the night, completely oblivious to her surroundings, it was just her and her painting and the view outside. As she began to paint the figure on the bench with the glow from the match that would illuminate the face and break up the darkness, Ayza noticed that in actual fact there was a woman sitting on the bench lighting up a cigarette. The figure blew out the match and Ayza could barely make out the outline backlit by streetlights as it turned to face Ayza.

Ayza caught her breath, and her fear turned to anger as she grabbed her keys and ran out into the park at this late hour to confront what she instinctively knew to be the source of the desecration of her paintings. The figure remained motionless on the bench watching Ayza run up to her, and then she stood up to face Ayza. Ayza in turn saw her own face reflected back at her in a black shroud of a shadow. She gasped as she felt life drain from her body, and the figure cackled and walked away.

The figure walked into Ayza's flat, cigarette dangling from her lips, and went up to the painting and started smudging out shapes in it to give it a more sinister look. The bewildered spirit of Ayza, trapped on the outside could now only look into her kitchen as she banged on the glass and screamed in silence while she watched her shadow-self take over her life. The doppelganger frowned at the spirit reflected in the glass, and raised a finger to her lips to quieten her.

Then laughed mirthlessly as she defaced the painting with monsters and spirits.

UNSEEN?

ROSE LEICESTER

I t was four o'clock in the morning and very quiet.

The nurse walked down the hospital corridor and failed to see the green lion that tried to bar her path. She walked right through it without turning a hair. She also did not notice the thirty-foot-long black python that slid along the floor, breathing fire that did not burn the walls – but it saw her. Purple bats flew about the nurse's head as she turned the corner and entered one of the wards.

A large, hairy, orange spider sat on the desk of the night sister as she wrote her reports. She reached for her cup of coffee and her hand went through the spider, which looked at her with its large black and yellow eyes.

"Ah, Nurse James," said the sister, "would you check on Tommy Wright? He's been having nightmares again."

The nurse went into the children's ward but found the little boy fast asleep, despite the red devil that sat on the edge of his bed, playfully poking him with a trident. She left him sleeping peacefully, although covered in wriggling blue maggots.

She walked knee deep through monsters of all shapes and sizes and myriad colours, crawling all over the floors and climbing up the walls. She was unaware of them all. *Not a soul moving,* she thought. *A nice, quiet night.*

In the secure room of a man suffering from delirium tremens, a pink elephant solemnly regarded the figure lying on the bed. Swarms of green bugs crawled onto the sheet that covered him. He opened his eyes – and screamed.

AN INFERNAL WONDER

OLIVE MALCOLM

Dark-robed figures chant the ancient ritual, their ghostly faces illuminated by guttering candle flame. The chapel is cold as the grave. The priest shivers with fear as black wings caress his face, clinging like treacherous spiders' webs, choking the prayer of deliverance on his chill lips. A tremor courses through his body like a lightning bolt, weakening his power to save the woman's tormented soul.

The sulphurous stench of evil lurks in dark corners, where light cannot penetrate. From deep within the womb of the sarcophagus, an unearthly keening bubbles up, ripping through the petrified hearts of the onlookers. Dull thuds beat against the leaden lid and the chains binding the coffin rattle and strain, as if assailed by an unseen, malevolent presence.

Clutching the rosary in trembling fingers, the priest intones, *'Ecce crucem Domini, fugite partes adversae.'* Behold, the cross of the Lord, begone all evil powers. Outside the storm rages, uprooting trees and toppling chimney pots. Dark clouds obscure the moon and the ghosts of the unshriven dead haunt the graveyard. The heavy oak door to the chapel, bolted and barred, threatens to give way as demons batter the sacred stronghold.

All night the forces of good and evil do battle; as dawn probes pale fingers through the east window, the foul apparitions melt away howling with rage, unable to withstand the revealing glare of day. Overcome with exhaustion, the priest slumps at the foot of the altar, his features ashen, eyes clouded with unearthly visions no human should ever have to witness.

On the second night the same thing happens. The solemn mass is sung, in accordance with the dying wishes of the old woman. Throughout her misspent and wicked life, she had been enslaved to the black arts of the devil. Growing old, she became fearful of the battering footsteps of death and longed for redemption. One day, a crow brought news of the death of her favourite son, the apple of her eye.

Prostrate with grief and wracked with pain, she summoned her remaining children – a monk and a nun – to her deathbed and begged them to save her from the cruel clutches of the Prince of Darkness. Hearing her desperate pleas, they agreed to do her bidding.

On the third night, the priest and his acolytes gather round the altar once more in trepidation. Clouds of incense spiral up into the bat-infested rafters like plainsong, and distorted shadows perform a *danse macabre* across the sanctuary walls, in grotesque parody of the pious prayers of the monks. Heads bowed in grief, the woman's children look on, as again their mother's spirit struggles to resist the savage enemy coming to claim her for eternity.

At midnight, the temperature drops and the air

thickens with a foul-smelling fog. The candles on the altar flicker and go out, as the heavy gold crucifix crashes to the ground. The priest's voice falters and an uneasy silence descends over the chapel.

With an almighty clap of thunder and a flash of lightning, the dark enemy arrives, shattering the wooden door and ripping it from its hinges. The monastery shakes to its foundations as a fearsome creature approaches the sarcophagus, calling the woman by name. The coffin lid is cracked open and the iron chains tossed aside as if weightless. As the woman is dragged by the hair from the chapel, screaming and cursing in terror, the monks stand rigid like stone effigies, their prayers strangled in their throats.

In the graveyard, a fierce black stallion tosses his head and stamps the frozen earth with massive hooves. Sharp iron spikes protrude from his broad back, gleaming menacingly. The woman's body, weak and helpless as a rag doll, is tossed onto the horse, the barbs tearing her vulnerable flesh to shreds. With a howl of triumph, the Prince of Darkness and his gruesome lackeys carry off their prize into the mist and beyond the rim of the world.

A lone crow perches on a crumbling headstone, close to the freshly dug grave waiting in vain to cradle the human remains of the hapless Witch of Berkeley. With a mocking caw, the crow casts a malevolent eye over the empty grave, spreads her wings and flaps off into the night sky, streaked with the first bloodstains of dawn.

Based on a story recorded by the 12th century historian, William of Malmesbury, concerning the chilling demise of the woman known as the Witch of Berkeley.

Was she really in thrall to the powers of evil, or just a harmless old woman suspected of sorcery? Various interpretations of her death are possible. Perhaps this was a tall tale told by a priest describing how an old woman was buried alive, but managed to break free and escape, or ...

AN ESCAPEE FROM THE PARISH

STUART SAMUEL

Shortly after moving to Leicestershire, I was entrusted with the care of three villages. They were only small, but the geography meant much travelling about, and everyone expected a visit from their vicar, whether they went to church or not. So with leading worship, visiting, preparation and the inevitable piles of paperwork back in the Rectory, life was very busy, but interesting and mainly fulfilling.

Occasionally, after one of those mornings which hadn't gone quite as well as I'd have hoped and I needed a break, I'd get in the Mini, flee the parish boundaries and head for the hills, in particular Charnwood Forest. Here there would be beautiful countryside, rolling hills and the occasional farm. After five or six miles, the object of my journeying would appear in the windscreen. The solid tower of Mount Saint Bernard Abbey, just beyond the driveway leading to the gatehouse.

The Abbey is a Cistercian Monastic Community, founded in 1835, and the first complete monastic community to be founded after the Reformation. Its order works hard every day with prayer, manual work and worship from rising at 3.15am for vigils to retiring at 8pm.

On entering the car park, there is a bookshop on the left, and facing you, the rose garden and behind that the majestic stone face of the Abbey. There might be some laughing and talking around the shop or people strolling through the gardens, but once in the Abbey, it is a different experience. The solid oak door closes with a satisfying clunk, leaving your nose greeted with the smell of polish and missals, and eyes adjusting from the sun outside to the comparative darkness, and peering into a vast chapel, with an altar in the middle and choir stalls behind and elegant columns either side. The general public is allowed up to the altar, but beyond that is the preserve of the members of the Order – an arrangement which makes sharing worship possible.

Upon entering, my senses were struck by three things.

The empty vastness of the place, with its simple and soaring architecture, the lingering smell of incense permeating the walls and woodwork even long after thurifer and acolytes had left, and the silence. Real, positive silence, not simply the absence of extraneous noise, but the sort of silence I could hear. Silence which permeated every space, both within me and without. These three combined to the grand sum of the holiness, or the otherness, of the place. A place where prayer has been offered for several generations. A place where some visitors would creep cautiously round, admiring the statues, others would find a corner and read, and others joined those generations in prayer on their knees.

I would simply sit there, soak up the atmosphere and feel my whole body relaxing, the tensions melting away, the cares and worries dropping into their correct perspective in the grand order of things in the re-imagining of the important.

I sometimes remembered a story my old Vicar at home used to tell. Of a man he found sitting at the back of his church every day.

"What are you doing?" he asked. "Every day I find you there. You don't seem to be praying, you're not reading or repairing the hymnbooks or something useful like that."

And the man replied, "I just sit and look at God ... And God just looks at me."

I'd just sit there, perhaps for an hour, perhaps longer – I never kept a record and never knew how long I'd been in there when I came out into the wide world again. But the vastness, the sense of deep, meaningful otherness and the silence remade me, ready to face the telephone's constant ringing and peoples' requests on my time with cheerfulness and enthusiasm.

SHE BATHES IN LIGHT

JENNY FINCH

Before you awake in the morning,
She takes up her basket and walks
Picking up jewelled orbs like candied fruits,
Shining bright where rain has oiled the street.
Sunshine breaking through stained glass
Dropping pools of colour at her feet.
Weather and clouds mirrored there,
On her stony path to elsewhere.

She bathes in light,
Her shadow's purple wine.
Cobwebs wet with raindrops,
Tangled through the vine.

It's a mystery to us in this town
How she brings such beauty to her door.
Does she follow the light or does it follow her?
Rainbow Queen, contemplating a sea of hues.
Cobalt glass, health giving water
Magic properties in medicine bottle blue.
She's drunk enough of this to know
Which parts of her are dangerous to show.

She bathes in light,
Her shadow's purple wine.
Cobwebs wet with raindrops,
Tangled through the vine.

Paint me in the Golden Hour, she begs,
When hot stone walls bake like sponge cake.
Cherry red scribbles frame the picture,
Shining bright through stems of Dogwood.
The best colours are fleeting, you can't hold them,
Perhaps they'd lose their beauty if we could.
Old masters hide away in darkened halls,
Hang my portrait on the whitest walls.

DARK DEEDS

JULIE WILTSHIRE

A semi-transparent voile spreads itself across the mantle of the earth and tracks the night. A curious moon plays peek-a-boo in the ghostly shadows of the witching hour. A flickering torch weaves its shining light through the spider webbed window of a man cave, teasing the blackness.

'I knew our old man had more than one, there Chris you take this one and I'll take the other.'

'I must be mad to listen to you. What if we get caught?

'Shh, keep you voice down, now let's get going.'

'You better keep your word about buying me a pint every night for a fortnight at our local,' whispers Chris.

'A week I said, don't try it on mate,' snaps Darren.

The two lads stumble across the sodden grass and load their spades into the back of the white van and speed off, leaving behind a trail of fog and a wandering throaty echo.

They arrive fifteen minutes later at iron gates surrounding St Arilda's Church. The youths stand like unwanted guests at the door. They ricochet their worried eyes around the silhouetted shadows of nothingness, maybe searching for Cerberus, the three- headed dog that lurks at the gates of Hell.

Darren swivels his head around and tosses Chris a blank stare who is by then fumbling to light a cigarette to calm his nerves. Chris struggles to hold on to it with his trembling fingers.

'Look mate I can't lose my job, I had to buy a black suit, and I've only had it for two weeks. A hundred quid the suit cost me from Burton's,' pleads Darren.

'You look a twat in it anyway. I've seen you, you look like a bouncer.'

'Great, great, look thanks for coming pal, but put that bloody fag out, let's have some respect.'

'Respect? That's rich coming from you,' sneers Chris.

'Anyway, you can smoke to your heart's content where we're going mate, it's all fire and brimstone,' chuckles Darren. 'And it's great that we've got spades because we'll sodding well need them.'

'It's not funny,' snaps Chris.

He stubs his cigarette out on a wooden post bleeding in the dampness. The iron gates before them are snug and the fences either side are weathered by winds and storms. Chris cracks the knuckles of his crude hands one by one and eyes up the tightly fitting gate before him.

'Look mate,' says Darren confidently,

Darren clasps his hands and Chris with his muddy trainers pushes himself through. Wriggling and squirming together like two overzealous ferrets in a hessian sack they finally conquer the gate.

Not wanting to offend the spirits they creep stealthily across the grass with their gear in their hands. They follow the flickering light of the torch that shines their way until they stumble across the freshly dug earth garlanded with lilies. Chris flings the lilies aside.

'Have some respect, you idiot, respect.'

'That's rich coming from you, plonker,' replies Chris.

Chris fiddles in his pocket.

'What are you doing, playing with yourself again?'

'No, it's my phone, you silly bugger, I'm trying to make a call.'

'Put it away, we haven't got time.'

'But you don't understand.' mutters Chris.

'Now what are you doing praying?'

Darren watches in astonishment as Chris drops to his knees with his head resting on the damp earth.

'I don't want to be wasting all my time on digging if you're wrong mate.'

Negative thoughts consume Chris, but out of loyalty he tries to dismiss them.

Complying with the tension in the air an owl hoots in the distance, which startles the pair and cracks open the insensitivity of their hearts. The full moon shows her smile once more, casting her glow on the damned.

Both muted lads begin digging the hallowed ground, and decide it is easier to live in their vacant head space and not let their heart space take over, it is safer that way. Deeper and deeper, they shovel staring blankly into the gaping mouth of the pit.

At last Darren hits something hard.

'We're here, we're here at last,' he cries.

They shovel the remaining earth away from the wooden lid and both lads with all their might wedge their spades under the rim and heave. The lid flings itself open and releases a stale odour. Both look away too afraid to stare death in the face and too afraid to look inwardly at their evil deeds. A flicker of guilt passes over them as they realise they have violated a woman's privacy. But as with youth it will leave no permanent scar.

'Oh God, I think I'm going to throw up' retches Chris casting his crazy bulbous eyes away from the coffin and into the blackness.

'We're going to Hell on a hand cart.'

'Is it there, Darren? Quick take a look, and let's bugger off.'

They pause for a second letting the silence drain from their dry mouths.

Darren shines the thin light down onto the shrouded bundle of putrefying flesh and bones, trying to avoid making contact with the windows of the dead woman's soul and runs the strange light from the torch up and down her frigid body.

'No, no, bloody Hell it isn't there, I can't believe it,' gasps Darren.

'What?' gasps Chris.

'You stupid bugger. Quick shut the damn lid and toss the earth back, and let's do a runner and get the Hell out of here.'

Chris crosses himself, why he didn't know, but he was taking no chances.

They work frantically consumed by the torment of their sins, whilst using their wit as a fork to stave off the simmering tension of their fears as they cannot embrace their uncomfortable thoughts which could swallow them up.

'What's that?'

'What?'

A whispering fills the air as a breeze picks itself up from the damp earth and flees across the graveyard away from the scene of the crime. The two miscreants momentarily freeze, and, stunned by their actions are too afraid to run towards or away from their fears. Death's watchmen of the night mock their shallow minds.

'For Christ's sake let's get out of here,' rasps Chris.

The dark stain of night once again snuffs out the moon. All that is left for the two lads to carry, besides their tools, is the heaviness of regrets and the weight of guilt.

The mists of misery engulf the two as they stumble from where they came and clamber over the crumbling wall.

They speed away in their white van and reach the local. Falling through the door and covered in mud the pair dive towards the bar.

'Line em up mate,' Darren faking his fearlessness, forcefully shouts, as his testosterone dissipates.

The barman looks quizzically at the two lads. What's wrong with you, you look like you've seen a ghost.

'If only you knew mate, if only you knew,' replies Darren.

Chris tosses Darren an unguarded glance. 'I'll never sleep again,' he whispers.

'You will when we've finished drinking in here mate,' replies Darren.

They both stand with cloven hooves side by side silently recalling their evil exploits. The barman pulls two pints of Doom. They grab at the frothing lifelines and drown their bubble brains in their beer.

The following morning Darren arrives at work. His boss has already beaten him to it and is busying himself in the parlour, whilst undertaking the solemn duties of the day.

'Ah, Darren, just the man I want to see.

'You know we were running headless yesterday I happened to find this on Mrs Johnson before I shut the lid. You must have dapped it down before you left. I knew she always liked to gossip but I feel this is beyond the pale.'

George chuckles to himself and passes the iPad to Darren.

'Don't leave it lying around next time you idiot. 600 quid you told me it cost. Having to replace it would have been the death of you.'

Darren stands in ghostly silence staring into space as he feels the serpent of shame slither down the chilling thoroughfare of his thoughts.

THE WITCH

REBECCA MCDOWALL

Her eyes are rumoured to be cold and black,
Far darker than a miner's sack,
A mere glance at them – not a second more,
And evil will befall your door.

Spells she'll cast all night long,
Her soft words a siren's sinful song,
Able to bend any man's wistful ear
To whisper his darkest fear

In the depths of Ashridge Forest,
You can hear the whispers of her coven chorus.
Tucked inside a rough wooden hut,
Under the full moon the night they disrupt.

Away from the villages they choose to meet,
Surrounded by deer, she needn't be discreet,
Guided by the moon they cast,
A sight that would leave hunters aghast.

Her wrinkles are a giveaway,
To the years spent casting off frigid ridgeways,
Her cauldron always simmering,
Its tempered sparks whispering.

So if you ask her if she is a witch,
Beware her ensnaring sales pitch.
Wondrous tales of herbs and flowers,
Infused with a coven's healing powers.

We do no harm she will protest,
Only treating the injured and distressed,
So if you come across her coven
Offer your thanks by the dozen

HOME TURF

J.J. DROVER

I woke with an uneasy feeling that something had pulled me from my sleep. I lay in the early silence of the pre-dawn morning listening intently for any noise that was not one of the familiar sounds of the house at this hour. Harriet sleeping deeply beside me, the clock ticking in the kitchen, a scurry of mice feet in the attic, a light pattering of rain on the window.

You grow accustomed to the regular noises of your home, hardly noticing them at times, often it is only in that eerie pre-dawn darkness that these everyday sounds amplify, become distinct and gain potential. But there was nothing out of the ordinary here now, in my mind I could map the house by these noises as I waited listening for something unfamiliar that might have woken me.

I doubted it would be one of the Xs, as we had become accustomed to calling them, they had become slow and sluggish at this time of year, and virtually never roamed at night, certainly not in a freezing rain like this one. They had become a little like reptiles or insects recently, most active and dangerous during the long hot summer days. In winter they could be found, if you really wanted to find them, huddled together shivering like a winter hive of honey bees, an endless pressing inwards to find warmth in the centre of the huddle. We had found one group like this last winter over at Carters Farm, there had been about thirty of them huddled pitifully in the back corner of the threshing barn trying to find shelter under some rotting bales of straw. I still don't quite know how I feel about dispatching them as I did. I tried to make it quick and painless, but deep down inside somewhere I still feel the shame and pity that they were once, or maybe at some level, still were human. But I also knew without doubt that as the weather warmed they would be out roaming the land once again, unfeeling, dangerous and diseased killers desperate to bite and tear us to pieces and consume our living blood. This land once had wolves roaming free in the wild places and the people then also knew the danger they posed was real and protected themselves in the only way they knew how.

In this weather, as I say, it was not the Xs that worried me as I lay there in bed that morning but something potentially worse. An incident had happened about a month ago that had unsettled our newfound equilibrium.

It's been five years since the first outbreak of Diabetes X, and in that time Harriet and I have built ourselves a small oasis of normality in what seemed to be a wild madness of chaos and destruction. We still have so many unanswered questions about what truly happened and why we were spared the infection, and I'm not sure we will ever find out now. To begin with we had no time to question, we only concentrated on lying low, surviving the storm that rolled around and over us like some biblical tempest. We clung to our Gloucestershire home like a raft, seemingly the only safe place in a wide unknown ocean. We held tight as best we could for that first year, truly unsure if we could, or if we wanted to survive, but something inside of us kept us going, waiting for a change, looking ever forward with hope that just around the corner life might return to some kind of normal again.

It was the spring of the following year that gave us some hope. The winter had been atrocious, I've never known one quite so cold or long. Harriet likened it to stories of the winter of '47 when flocks of sheep were found frozen in the fields, snow drifts covered houses and rural communities were cut off for months.

We had a pretty tough time of it but we pulled through, and with the welcome arrival of spring we turned our thoughts to growing food and making good our home. We had no idea of where anybody else was or where we should go, the power was out and with it all communication with the outside world. The Xs were abroad again and in greater numbers towards our local towns and cities it seemed. We made a few tentative attempts at surveying the lay of the land beyond our immediate area in hope of finding some element of society but outside of the relative safety of our home there seemed to be only the chaos of this unknown disaster and so we decided to stay. This was our home after all and we wanted to stay if we could.

We began to use the local farmsteads and houses we

knew well as climbers and explorers used base camps and advance posts, fortifying them and leaving caches of food and essential supplies so that if we were away from the house, we knew we could take refuge if needed. This gave us the advantage of being able to move a little bit about our area in some safety and as a bonus to use a number of spectacular walled gardens and greenhouses that belong to the larger houses in the neighbourhood.

We genuinely felt as if we were living some fantastical dream or hallucination at times. Nearly everyone had watched a movie, or TV series, or read a book about the zombie apocalypse, and I think most of us had formed some kind of strategy that we would employ as the hero to save the day. But the reality was just so overwhelming, this just shouldn't be happening in our own beautiful Cotswolds, it just didn't seem possible. And yet here we were living that very story for real.

And so about a month ago, Harriet and the dogs were away from the house for the afternoon. She had gone down to the old manor in the village, harvesting winter greens and beetroot we had grown in the big walled garden.

I was busy at home in the kitchen sorting through a sack of potatoes from the pantry that had begun to give off a faint odour of mildew, meaning a bad potato was in the bag which could spoil the lot if not removed. I heard a noise behind me, turned and was brought face to face with a couple of serious looking men. I had a brief and momentary realisation that they were uninfected before the tougher looking of the two pushed me quite violently back against the cupboard which I hit with a crash and fell to the floor. They were not gentle as they rough-handled me across the kitchen and propped me up in a chair, tying my hands behind my back.

They were pirates through and through, here to rob and plunder our precious stores. Why they didn't kill me straight off I still don't know, most probably they were inclined to a little sport or thought they could extract useful information about the area. They had the air of those that had done this before which I found interesting, meaning that there were almost certainly more of us homesteaders out there, keeping to the areas they knew, just like us making good as best they could.

These two intruders were I think about to begin their questioning when to my relief, and to their surprise, a quiet but determined order of "Hands up!" was issued from behind them. Then a small burp of laughter followed this command. It came from Harriet who was standing in the kitchen doorway, bright eyed and grim faced with a shotgun held firmly at waist height, pointing straight towards the men. A moment of confusion hung in the air for a brief moment before the tougher one reached for a pistol he had in his belt that was met with an almighty ear splitting explosion as the shotgun fired once and then a second time as the other man also made a move toward her.

Harriet had used the gun before, but not like this. The room was deathly quiet for a moment after the deafening blasts, though I think actually all I could hear was the ringing in my ears.

We found each other's gaze and in that moment we knew that this was something new but something we had also feared from the start. Oddly though it also brought a brief glimmer of hope as we later realised that if they had found us, then perhaps we could also find others just like us.

Later that evening Harriet and I discussed the events of the afternoon and the potential implications it had. Harriet, as I said, had been away from the house when the men had arrived but had fortunately been alerted to their arrival before me. The sound of a vehicle had drifted into the walled garden, and for a while she didn't quite know what to make of it. Such a long time had passed since we had heard any motor vehicle that the very notion of them had somehow been misplaced. But the sudden recollection and realisation that it was a car driving past the walled garden and on up the lane towards our house gave her a momentary jolt of panic, quickly replaced by relief that at last we were obviously not alone!

She dashed to the garden gate that led to the lane and was just in time to see the old Land Rover rumble past. There was something in the demeanour of the occupants that brought her up sharp, the terribly grim looks on their faces, she said, that held her back for a moment from dashing out onto the lane to wave them down. A fortunate moment indeed it turned out.

The feeling of panic returned followed this time by fear, and so she armed herself with a shotgun and leaving the dogs in the garden lest they break her cover,

Harriet made her way up the lane to the house.

She realised her fear was well founded when the Land Rover stopped a few hundred yards from the house and she watched the men climb out and make their way stealthily on foot towards the house, one going right the other left, one to the front and the other slipping around the back. This wasn't a friendly visit.

The rest she said was just a case of following them without being seen, though there was a point when she was peeking through the kitchen window and saw their rough treatment of me that she nearly blew her cover in indignant outrage, but keeping calm she instead crept around and came into the drama unseen from behind.

Harriet paused for a moment in her account of the events, she smiled and with a small laugh she continued to recount how in the midst of this deadly game she had nearly called out 'hands down, this is an up stick!' as though she were in some bizarre comedy film scene.

I knew now that this was actually what had woken me this morning – the knowledge that there were others out there, not just others like those men, those marauders, but others like ourselves, perhaps even some semblance of a society. We knew we had to leave, but we also knew that to leave our home would mean stepping out into the unknown again.

Our recent feeling of security came from our sense of place, our familiarity with this small island of hope we had clung to and lived off over the past few years. This night, there were none of the unknown, unfamiliar sounds here that had woken me this morning and so I settled deeper under the covers and drifted back into sleep.

I would need the rest for tomorrow we would begin our search for a new home.

The 'Diabetes X' short story series by J.J. Drover begins in Spooky Ambiguous *(published 2022, Crumps Barn Studio)*

THE THUNDER AND LIGHTNING ARE IN US

NIKOLINA HUA

Doffing at all the inscrutable curtains I see, hat falls
upon this gentlewoman. Undisciplined eyes sheathing
me a rake – armed with swords.
Each time where the rock peaks, I sit and clutch,
        fingers draw and rub into self-portrait:
Dueling of swords from different hands,
        snorting a realm, consisting
of my lungs from right to left; each time I swallow
the fuse from organs of different men:
        drawing back, blaze,
decease and revive, sending sneers and didactic
        summons beneath their Damocles pikes,
lying on me like ruthless revenge. A bad woman
        worth no soft touch
onto her infant-like flower which contains
        Rousseau's tear!
They do not know a woman who guides tigers,
        I am fiercer than wolves through
salt water within two cat's eyes until my only
        freshness, he sees,
at the end of a dusky lecture and a clutching of
        the polemic body.

About how furious I can roar during a poisonous
        climax; we lower our swords
when the first summer rain drops come with the
        force of May.
And there is thunder for me to slip out of
        a virgin world
From time to time. I swallow as if I have never
        swallowed anyone before,
When you stand among thunder and lightning –
        they are more salient
than any god or saviour between animals and humans.
Finally, I know I have been missing, the lion inside
        your amber eyes
and your every step pounders an ebbing wave into
        my desolated moor,
Mushrooming, a spring wind ascends to the downhill,
        splits me wide awake
– a diminished gluttony, a virgin reincarnates
        when she loves again

A WINTER'S FAIRYTALE

AMARIS CHASE

There was something sinister about trees in winter, thought Cerys as she entered the forest. The trees that stood forlorn of leaves had branches reaching out like evil tendrils, scraping her cheeks, tugging at her hair. Her bare limbs tried to dodge the nettles and brambles and she struggled to avoid becoming entangled with the ivy. The frost-bitten earth was chilling her feet through her threadbare shoes, but the physical pain was nothing like the pain she would endure if she was not successful with her quest. Cerys was but a young girl, not quite old enough to work in the mills, and already like a mother to her three much younger siblings who were mere babes themselves.

Cerys' father had died the previous year, and the burden of care fell to her mother alone, and now her mother lay bedridden, pale and gaunt with the sweating sickness. Even at her tender age, Cerys knew that her mother had days, if not hours, left to live.

She remembered with a pang in her heart the last conversation that she had had with her mother earlier that afternoon.

"Go to the darkest part of the forest, right at its heart, where no birds sing, no animals enter, and where the wind cannot blow. You will find ferns that light up the dark, and beneath those ferns you will find the herbs that will cure me." Her mother stopped to take some water as Cerys mopped her brow. "Remember not to offend the forest spirits. The dark heart of the forest has goblins, fairies, spirits both good and bad. Trust no one, talk to none of them if they challenge you, just walk away from them calmly. If they sense your fear, they will claim you. Hurry child, I cannot hang on much longer." She was reduced to a whisper by now, and with that, her mother turned to her side to sleep off her exhaustion.

Cerys didn't know what it meant to be 'claimed' by a spirit, or fairy, or goblin but understood it wasn't a good thing. She tended to her siblings and promised to return before nightfall, but that they mustn't leave the house, and they must continue mopping their mother's brow.

Cerys ran to the forest as fast as she could – the forest she had always been wary of, the forest that seemed to be forbidding, and the ill-ease she felt at being surrounded by trees that appeared to be watching her. The forest was full of beech and birch trees that looked as if they had eyes and mouths embedded in their trunks, which were in fact part of their natural form, but to a young child these lesions and marks were 'faces' in the trees. It was through these faces that Cerys could navigate her way through the dense forest.

At the periphery of the forest was a slim birch tree with dark oval rings protruding through the white trunk which to Cerys looked like the face of a woman with thick pouting lips, almost disapproving of those entering the forest. Further behind this birch was the thicker trunk of a beech tree that had one angry looking eye and a crooked mouth shape which reminded Cerys of a one eyed ogre from a story her dad used to tell her.

Beyond the ogre tree was another birch tree with a low branch that reached upwards, and it had an almost startled expression with two dark ovals for eyes and a more rounded lesion that looked like a mouth in shock. To Cerys, the tree looked like it had been caught by surprise and was about to surrender to someone. The forest was full of these birch trees, each tree having its own unique expression that Cerys used to remember the best places to forage for edible greens, mushrooms, and where to lay traps for small animals. For despite her sense of unease in the forest, her family were dependent on it for firewood, for furniture, cooking utensils, repairs to the cottage, food. Without the forest, they could not survive, and now with her mother on her deathbed, she had never needed the forest more than she did now.

She listened keenly to the sounds of the forest and the songs of the birds. As the snapping of twigs and the sound of scampering animals began to decline, the sounds of birds became more sporadic, and the forest became darker, she knew she was approaching the heart of the forest. She had never been this deep before, fearful of the darkness at its heart. Her legs now ached in the bitter cold despite sweating from running, and Cerys felt an odd sensation that someone was right behind her, but every time she turned around to check, all she could see was the menacing gazes of the trees.

The light was fading fast as the winter evening approached. The forest seemed to have become darker with evergreen trees that Cerys didn't recognise, creating a thick canopy of leaves through which light struggled to pass. She didn't know which way to run, her mother hadn't told her, but she understood that she had to go deeper still. She had to trust that she would find her way home. The forest was still, she could hear no sound now except the scraping of her feet, the percussion of her heart throbbing violently, and her rapid breathing.

She was now alone and frightened in a part of the forest that was unfamiliar to her, but she reminded herself that however scared she was of the forest, the thought of losing her mother was much more terrifying.

Finally, in the distance, she saw a faint green glow. Could it be a forest spirit waiting to claim her? As she drew closer to the light, she realized it was coming from a whole patch of luminous green ferns, just as her mother described. At last! She could grab the herbs and run back in the direction she came.

But just as she felt underneath the first fern, she was startled to hear a snoring noise. She looked around and saw that on the other side of the ferns stood a heavily creviced tree, and at the base of the trunk the crevices mapped out two crescent shapes for sleeping eyes with thick brows, below which was a flowing wooden moustache in the same texture of the trunk, and just below this was a smooth round stump, perhaps where a root had been cut off. The tree shook gently with each snore. A tree spirit!

Cerys gingerly plucked the herbs as quietly as she could, not wanting to wake the tree spirit. Just as she had finished and had turned around to tiptoe away, she heard a thunderous yawn, the ground shook, and a bellowing voice rang out into the darkness, "Wait! Who is trespassing on my land?"

Cerys froze in fright! She nearly dropped the herbs, and the shock of being spoken to by a tree meant that she completely forgot her mother's warning not to speak to any magical entity. She turned around slowly and resolved to beg the tree to let her go. Tears streamed down her flushed cheeks and she pleaded, "Forgive me kind spirit, my mother lies at home on her deathbed, and I must make haste with these herbs or her fever will not break!"

"Kind?" said the spirit mockingly. "Kind?" And then in a softer tone he said, "And what will you give me in return for taking from my property? If you take from the forest, you must give something in return, otherwise there will be no balance between human and nature."

"Please Kind Spirit, we are a poor family, we have nothing of value to give you in return." Cerys felt her heart sink. She had failed her mother, she had failed her siblings. She began to sob in despair.

"You think you can take from the forest and give nothing back?" bellowed the tree spirit. "The forest must always be kind to you and yet you are not kind to the forest! It is tree spirits like me who protect the forest from the likes of you!" he cried angrily.

Then he changed to a more placid tone, "However, you are here on a noble cause, I suppose ..." He almost smiled.

Cerys stood nervously, waiting for what he would do to her. She heard a snapping and creaking sound and felt a scratching sensation on her ankles. She looked down and gasped as she saw black tendrils of the tree's roots slowly entwine themselves around her feet and pierce into her skin. She looked again at the tree spirit fearfully.

"Don't worry," he laughed mockingly, "I am not going to hurt you. You take from the forest, and you give back to the forest." Cerys didn't understand what he meant, she only understood she was not going to be free of the tree spirit.

"Go and give your mother the herbs. Go now!"

And with that, the roots untangled themselves from her feet and sank back into the earth. Cerys had not a moment to lose, she spun around and ran for dear life whilst still clutching the herbs to her chest. She ran aimlessly, hoping to see the birch and beeches that she knew so well but the darkness was never ending, and she crashed into one tree after another whilst at the same time she could hear the creaking of the soil breaking behind her as the roots of other trees followed her, other tree spirits laughing behind her ...

But then a Will-o'-the-wisp appeared before her – a warm glow of friendly light – and she understood it would guide her out of the forest. She followed the ball of light, darting in and out of the trees until at last she reached the edge of the forest.

Despite feeling drained of energy, Cerys wasted no time in getting back to the cottage and was greeted with desperate hugs by her confused and frightened siblings. She first checked on her mother – she was still breathing, but almost unconscious. Cerys boiled down the herbs to make them more digestible and fed them to her mother in one tentative spoonful after another.

She felt relief as she watched colour return to her mother's cheeks, and eventually her mother smiled weakly at her.

"You came back, my child!" Her mother reached out to squeeze Cerys's hand in thanks, but as her cold palm rested on the child's hand, she frowned, and then her eyes widened in horror.

"No!" She gasped, for she was too weak to scream.

Puzzled, Cerys pulled back her hand and saw her hand had become deformed with nodules and splinters breaking through the skin. Her veins had started to turn into branches. Cerys stepped back in shock, looked at both hands, and then her feet, which were also morphing into parts of a tree. The siblings shrank back from her.

"Noooooo!!!!"

Cerys let out the scream that her mother had been unable to muster. She ran out of the cottage, screaming and crying, angry at her fate. She had to find the tree spirit again and beg to be allowed to stay with her family longer! Her mother needed her! She had only run into the forest a few moments when she suddenly felt pulled to the earth, like a magnetic force she couldn't fight. She felt a piercing pain that forced her arms up, branches sprouting through her limbs …

In her mind were the words of the tree spirit. "You take from the forest, and you give back to the forest … You belong to the forest now."

And now when you enter the forest, you will find a new birch tree with lesions that look like downcast eyes and open mouth, like a person sobbing angrily.

GARDEN DIVINE

DAPHNE DENLEY

I'm a sprite, not a fairy, pixie, imp or elf
I live by the pond and the trees by myself
I've fingers that fire, no need for a wand
Spells only kind, for healing what's wrong
People normally don't see me, as invisible can be
I dart through the sky so very quickly indeed
I really don't mind you gardening, no
But this is my home, only place that I know
Cut down the reeds, the branches and trees
Then nowhere to hide, in weather extremes
I chase off white butterflies and pests from
     your crops
Make my clothing, pruning flower petals and tops
Pesky a bit, but my intentions are good
And only ride your cat, when it plays in the woods
Put sticky honey and rotting apples in the trees
It's attracted many glow-worms, like fairy light beads
I go invisible sometimes, just to tease and surprise
Tickle you with my wings, so you sneeze
     wondering why
I'm only friends with the sprites, however you
     I quite like
Secret keep yours and mine, in this garden divine?

SOUTHWOLD FERRY

CERI VYNER

We had decided, my mother and I, to spend a day in Southwold, a lovely little town on the Suffolk coast. We walked up the attractive High Street, looking in the shop windows at anything interesting, browsed for a while in the antique centre, bought a cake at the bakery and spent some time admiring the beautiful church with its exterior of knapped flint work, before walking over the common. We wandered down to the river and watched the yachts being moored to the wooden jetties that arched over the water. Nearby was the Blackwater pub where we ate a fish and chip lunch, served in wrapped paper at the outdoor tables, from which we were able to admire the beautiful view across the common to the town and lighthouse beyond.

After lunch we sauntered over the bailey bridge to the rival parish of Walberswick to look around there. At about four o'clock we wandered back down to the harbour mouth where the ferryman was waiting to row people over to the Southwold side of the river. Two or three people were already in the bow of the boat so the ferryman handed my mother and I into the stern seating us on opposite sides to balance the boat. The ferry boat was moored at right angles to the shore so that I had a view along the coast of the distant rooftops and church tower of Walberswick.

It was a beautiful sunny afternoon, but as I looked along the shore I could see patches of mist, river mist I thought. The air was rather hazy all of a sudden, so it was a minute or two before I noticed a dark figure running along the tow path towards the ferry. The tow path consisted of a muddy, slippery track with tufts of grass ready to trip up the unwary. Anyone running there risked a broken ankle, so I assumed the person was in a real hurry to catch the ferry, but at that moment the ferryman prepared to unhitch the boat.

'Hang on a minute, someone else is coming,' I informed him. I turned to look and saw the figure, nearer now and with a smaller figure running beside him. We waited. After several minutes the ferryman looked at me. 'Are they coming?' he said.

'Yes, they'll be here soon.'

'Where are they?' demanded my mother, turning to look, 'I can't see anybody!'

I peered into the misty distance; at first I couldn't see anything, then faintly through the mist patch I saw the figures again. 'Oh, there they are.' I exclaimed. 'I can see them.'

'Oo are they?' demanded the ferryman.

I looked. 'There's a man and a child,' I replied.

'What's 'e wearing?' the ferryman suddenly looked worried.

The two figures were still running towards us.

'The man's wearing a black coat and the child's ... wearing black too.' My voice faltered as I realised the strangeness of this, no-one dressed children in black these days. The ferryman suddenly seemed very agitated and began to untie the rope.

'Aren't you going to wait; they'll be here any minute?' I asked in a puzzled voice.

'There ain't no room!' muttered the ferryman angrily.

'Yes there is, they can sit here.' I patted the empty seat next to me.

We were suddenly interrupted by my mother. 'Where are they? I thought you said they were just coming?'

'They were here a minute ago. They must've run behind the ferry hut.' I replied in an astonished voice. 'Didn't you see them?'

'No, well, I thought I saw something, but when I looked again, there was nothing there,' remarked my mother, sounding puzzled.

I turned to look along the shore. There was nobody; the shingly beach beside the river, the marshes, the distant village, could all be clearly seen in the bright sunlight, but of the man and boy running towards us there was no sign.

'Where've they gone?' I asked. 'They must've been running for the ferry, the path's too slippery to be just running.'

The ferryman hastily unhitched the boat, tossed the rope down onto the planks and grasped the oars. Quickly he sat down and began to row. After a few strokes he steadied the boat and turned to me.

'Can you see them now? '

I looked along the shore. 'No … wait! Yes!' I replied. 'There they are, up there.'

'Where are they?' asked the ferryman.

'Beside the ferry hut,' I said.

'I can't see them,' said my mother in a shocked voice.

On the shingle bank behind us stood a tall, grim-faced, bearded man in black fisherman's oilskins and sou'wester. His left arm rested on the shoulders of a small boy of about six, also in dark clothes. Both figures stared unblinkingly at the ferry boat.

'Do you know who they are?' my mother asked the ferryman.

'I knows them! They never cross!' was his reply. Then he turned to me with an anxious look, 'Are they still there? ' I nodded. 'What're they doin'?' he demanded.

'Watching,' I replied, 'just watching us!' I could see them as clearly as I see my friends and colleagues. Luckily, the ferryman had his back to us and my mother did not see, but as the ferry boat pulled out into the river, the ghostly sou'westered figure and the boy, who had been watching us, climbed silently into the ferry boat and sat down in the place next to me, the place I had indicated earlier, only this time their outlines were faint and less distinct than before. I could see through them.

'This ain't your business,' muttered the ghostly man, looking sternly in my direction.

I stared aghast as they sat beside me. Their grim presence disturbed me deeply, so that I leaned right over the side of the boat to get away as far as possible.

Shaking with silent terror, I gripped the side of the boat with white knuckles. A feeling of utter dread overwhelmed me. I felt as if a lead doughnut had settled in my stomach.

My first thought was that the ferry was going to sink and that we would drown. The river is close to the harbour mouth here and the currents are treacherous. My mother, who was unaware of our strange companions, was critical of the way I was sitting.

'Sit up, dear! I don't know why you're leaning over like *that!*'

Suddenly, when we reached the centre of the river, the great weight in my stomach lifted, and I knew even before I turned to look, that they had gone; I breathed a heartfelt sigh of relief and willed the Southwold shore nearer.

In a few more minutes we had reached the other side and the ferryman hastily tied the boat up and handed people out. I stumbled out of the boat, my legs shaking as I walked up the jetty. There was a long queue of people waiting to be ferried back, but I heard the ferryman tell them curtly:

'I ent goin' back fer at least fifty minutes! You'll 'ave ter wait!'

He was clearly very upset and I watched him stomping off to a nearby fisherman's hut.

I have long since wished that I had gone after him and questioned him about the figures, but my mother was with me and the opportunity was lost. Other people must have seen them, the ferryman obviously knew who they were and was alarmed by their presence.

All I know is that earlier that afternoon I had stood before the memorial in Walberswick church, dedicated to a former ferryman who, together with his small grandson, was drowned when their ferryboat sank during a sudden storm. *Poor souls* I thought as I read the inscription, poor *souls!* I think they used my energy to revisit the scene of their tragedy and I have never dared to go over the ferry since.

TO THE RED BEACONS

NIKOLINA HUA

In grand waves shivers sail – away from the earth.
The edge where briny voices are the crests, ride
at my reflection. Anchors, sharp ritual of the
        wavering night.

I face an inscrutable vision: plumes of fire ruffled by
        their watery rhythms –
Or is it now a waking dream that sobs beneath
        crimson swamps?
The visions are always figments,
        water-bodies and mothers
directing mud over my untidy skin.

If the sensations (breathing in and out
        in two short spaces)
            are what I find serene, I am yet to convict,
to be derided by the polar grace ahead.
As the celestial forces in the sky
draw back with fear inside their sphere,
those febrile solstices are desperate on butterfly's spirals
when their effulgent wings are pinched on walls
under the pale moonlight.

Now here, the silence awaits. How secluded,
        a drained hermit in
worldly dust under her lotus feet, red beacons are too
        hot for the earth. Dance!
            They
                lost
                    utterly ———— unstable,
sacrificing their lustrous hues atop each
        thunderous climax
of fleeting waves, weighing the years
        but abnormally lively.
A fist twists its darkish veins, effusively signalling

the taps within a nymphal heart after hundreds of
        times when a body rots
in terrible silence, in the inner sea of desolated lands.
The distraction of solitude, however,
never jades the mirror of my face, and only
        greets me passionately.
Such red-blooded, such unbending, watery feathers,
when was the last time this animalistic
        apparition ascended?
Eyes to eyes,
they mottle the waves, reincarnating in their warm,
        ripening souls.

But the red beacons remain timeless.
    The mother laughs,
quivering against the daylight during its
    beckoning march:
You are ridiculously frail …
      You cannot rope the will.
        You cannot ride the colour!
For a reflection
that sees her body as a bind, she is vowing
    the most miraculous thing
in horrible solitude and blazing through
    the abyss between
two glows, equally merry
amidst the presence of the wonderful Divine.

THE DOLLHOUSE

VICKI FLETCHER

'Home sweet home!'

Karina is beaming as she unlocks the front door to the house – *our* house. We haven't been married long, just three short months, and this house is our first together. We didn't mind the condition it was in when the estate agent showed us around. We like a challenge.

We move our belongings in quickly. We don't have too much, deciding to update our furniture when the house is more complete. Mango, our jack russell-cross-something, trots around the lower floor, sniffing everything and checking that this new place we've brought him to is up to muster. He flops in front of an ancient, unlit fireplace, and promptly falls asleep. I smile at him, my arms filled with small boxes of knick-knacks and kitchenware I'm trying to find a corner to store in. It seems the house has passed his inspection.

We order in that night, neither of us up to sifting through boxes to try and cook in the new kitchen. The doorbell rings and Karina leaps up to go answer. She comes back moments later with a mildly puzzled expression on her face, pizza boxes stacked in her hands.

'He left it on the doorstep,' she says, kneeling on the rug with me and Mango and setting down our first meal in the new house. 'He'd already left by the time I got there.'

'Weird,' I say, taking a bite and burning my tongue on the cheese.

'They never did that in the city,' Karina muses, opening her own box.

'Different rules out here, I suppose.'

She nods, her mouth full, and we turn our attention fully to eating. When we are stuffed to the point of exploding, we trudge to the mattress we've dragged into what will one day be our master bedroom and fall asleep, still fully dressed but heads full of excitement for the adventure this house promises to bring us.

The first few weeks in our new home are exhausting, but fun. We begin the arduous task of renovating the house, stripping old wallpaper and prising up ancient, musty carpet that no amount of cleaning will ever save. The old staircase needs new steps, which we discover when carrying down an armful of rubbish to be binned from upstairs and my foot goes clean through one of them. I manage to keep my balance, somehow, and wrench my foot free with no injury. We call a man to come replace them, but he can't fit us in for a few weeks, so every time we climb the staircase is nerve-wracking, images of tumbling right through at the forefront of our minds as we count down the days to his arrival. Until then, we are careful.

Karina begins her new job at the four-week mark. I work from home, so I have more time to potter around and do odd jobs when she is away. I am up in the attic, storing things we won't need until the house is ready, when I find it: a small door, hidden behind boxes the old owner left behind.

I try the handle. It turns, and then stops. Locked. At first I'm disappointed, but then I remember the keyring the estate agent gave us. There was a small brass key that neither of us could figure out the purpose for. Cleaning forgotten, I climb down the ladder and head to the kitchen, where we have hung the keyring on a hook beside the back door. The brass key is there, tiny and shiny. New-looking.

Back up the ladder, I try the key on the little door, and to my immense satisfaction it works.

'Ha!' I exclaim, and now my mind is full of childish excitement. What is behind the door? Treasure? Hidden antiques we could sell for a fortune? *Treasure?!*

The reality is nothing quite so glamorous. I stoop to get through the door, cough and sneeze as years of dust are disturbed and sent flying, and blink in the gloom. The room is small, just like the door. It feels like an afterthought – built by someone long after the house was constructed, and cramped for it. I look around, hoping to find that childish treasure, but there is nothing.

Then my eyes fall on a lumpy shape in the back corner. Correction, I think. Something! It is concealed by an old motheaten sheet. I toe it uncertainly, then grasp a corner and pull it up, sending even more dust flying into the air. I reel back, arms over my face, and then look at what it is I've found.

It's a dollhouse, built to look like this house

in miniature. I am instantly captivated. It has an intricately decorated exterior that looks like the house exactly, with the beautiful red door we fell in love with at first sight. It even has the brass knocker. The front of the dollhouse is on hinges and I carefully open it up, revealing the inside. Every room is represented in absolute detail, but as I look, glancing from room to room, a sense of disquiet falls over me. The dollhouse is our house exactly. Exactly. The step where my foot went through is broken, a small hole punched through the wood. Miniature boxes are piled in the living room, exactly where I placed them when we first moved in. Wallpaper has been stripped from the walls, and carpets have been removed to reveal old wooden floorboards. There is a tiny mattress laying on the floor of the master bedroom – even the suitcase we have been living out of as we get the built-in wardrobe fixed up.

I glance at the living room again. On a tiny version of our rug is a small wooden dog. Somehow I know that if I were to go back downstairs I would find Mango there, asleep on the real rug. In the attic is another wooden doll, this one red-headed and wearing my clothes. There is no doll representing Karina, but I wonder if, when she returns, there will be.

I place the sheet back over the dollhouse, lock the room with the tiny brass key, and return the keyring to its hook by the door. I busy myself with little chores around the place, trying to push the dollhouse from my mind. Failing.

Karina returns and we make dinner together, eating

in front of the fireplace as has become the norm. My thoughts linger on the dollhouse upstairs. I can feel it there, like a pressure from above. I wonder who built it, and why. I wonder if the previous occupant knew about it. I wonder how it works. Karina asks me what I'm thinking about and I almost tell her, and then for some reason don't. I'm not sure why. Perhaps I think she'll think it silly. We spend the weekend working on the master bedroom together, trying to get at least one room done. By Sunday night it looks great; fresh paint and new flooring, and a very attractive bed frame we bickered over putting together, make the room complete.

I don't return to the dollhouse until three days later, though it has been ever-present in my thoughts. It's Monday and Karina has gone back to work, and while I don't think I'm trying to keep it a secret from her, for some reason I wait for her to leave before venturing into the attic again. The sheet comes off, the dollhouse is revealed, and I let out a deep breath I didn't know I was holding. It has changed slightly. Doll-me is wearing the clothes I am wearing today; Mango is in the master bedroom, asleep on the bed. The new bed.

Inspiration strikes me. I rummage in my pockets, looking for something – anything. I come up with a penny, old and tarnished, and, after a moment's thought, place it in the attic of the dollhouse. I hold my breath, turn. Exit the small door. I cast my eyes around and see nothing; just dust and boxes, and footprints where I have walked through. Then, something glints in the dim light. I walk to it, dreamlike, and stoop. When I stand back up I have a penny in my hands, old and tarnished. When I return to the dollhouse, my penny has vanished.

I decide to conduct another test. Hurrying downstairs I find a tin of paint, half-used and not enough left to do anything worthwhile with. I grab it and a small paintbrush and return to the attic, where I prise the tin open with a small screwdriver. It's a soft blue inside – Karina's favourite colour. I dip in the paintbrush, scrape off the excess, and lean into the dollhouse. I'm not sure what I'm doing, not sure whether it will work or if I'm just imagining things, but I begin to paint the spare room anyway, splashing paint around until the walls are completely covered. A few drops get onto the wooden floorboards but I don't really notice; they're going to be carpeted over anyway. I put the paintbrush aside and glance inside the tin. It's still almost half-full. If this works …

I leave the tin where it is and climb back down the ladder. Mango glances at me as I pass the master bedroom but lays back down when he realises I'm not coming to fuss him. I reach the end of the corridor, where the spare bedroom is. The door is closed and I pause, uncertain, but it doesn't last long. I grasp the doorknob and twist, pushing it open and stepping in.

The room is blue – soft blue. Karina's favourite colour. I stand there, hand on the doorknob, mouth agape. Droplets of paint scatter the floorboards in exactly the spots they did in the dollhouse. I enter, still not believing what I'm seeing. The walls are shiny and I touch one, coming away with blue fingertips. It's still wet.

My mind is reeling. I check the time and realise Karina won't be back for another four hours. Plenty of time to surprise her, I think, a plan suddenly forming. I collect everything I think I'll need – rolls of wallpaper, tins of fresh paint, small swatches of carpet - and carry them upstairs. Then I go rooting around some of the boxes I've placed in what will be my studio. I find my crafting materials in the last box I check, naturally, and add them to the pile to be transported to the dollhouse room. There, I set to work.

'What the—' Karina stops mid-sentence, her eyes bulging, her mouth hanging open.

'Surprise!' I say, standing at the bottom of the stairs. The step has been repaired and new carpet laid. The walls are cloaked in wallpaper and tiles have been laid in the entryway. Beyond, the living room is bright and airy, the paint Karina having chosen working wonderfully on the walls. The only thing missing is new furniture, and only because I ran out of time.

'How …?' she asks and I smile, tapping the side of my nose and saying nothing. She drops her bag to the floor and begins to explore our fully renovated home. Walls, floors – everything is fresh and new. She enters the kitchen and can't help but laugh with delight, and I follow her, watching her, smiling at her joy. My heart swells as she runs up the stairs and laughs with delight at the completed bedrooms, study, bathroom.

'How!' she repeats, a statement not a question, and I barely have time to open my arms before she throws herself into them. 'This must have cost a fortune,' she says, suddenly concerned, and I shake my head, reassuring her.

'Barely a penny,' I say and she glances around in wonder, before appraising me.

'But you're not even dirty,' she murmurs, taking one of my hands and studying it. 'There's no paint or anything. How did you do this?'

'Come with me.'

Up the ladder we go, through the cobwebs and dust. I produce the tiny brass key from my pocket, detached now from its keyring, and place it in the lock. I bend to stoop through the door and Karina follows me, frowning. I lead her to the back of the room, grasp the sheet and pull it off, like a magician executing a trick. When she sees the dollhouse, she gasps.

'It was this,' I say quietly, kneeling beside her. The dollhouse is pristine. Perfect. The only thing left to do is the exterior, and I left that for last so Karina wouldn't be tipped off when she arrived home. She glances from room to room; this one wrapped in the wallpaper she picked out months ago, that one in the paint I liked the most. Tiny tiles have been laid in the entryway and kitchen – that was tricky, I remember, but worth it – and even the wardrobes and cupboards have had a fresh lick of paint to bring them back to life. In the attic, two dolls dressed as us – one red-headed, the other blonde –

kneel by an even tinier version of the dollhouse.

She turns to me, uncomprehendingly, and I explain. I explain the broken stair, the wallpaper, the penny. I explain the tiny figure of Mango, of us. I explain bringing paint and wallpaper up here, renovating the dollhouse in just a matter of hours and returning downstairs to find it mirrored in reality too. She's shaking her head. She can't believe what I'm saying, but she can't refute it either. She saw downstairs; she knows I couldn't have possibly done it all myself in just a few short hours.

'It's incredible,' she whispers and I nod, grinning as I take in my handiwork, proud. 'Incredible.'

Then she reaches out a hand and does what I have never dared to do. Before I can stop her, before I can even speak a word of protest, she plucks the tiny figure of herself out of the attic. I turn to her, everything in slow motion.

The doll exits the dollhouse and disintegrates, falling from between Karina's fingers and vanishing amongst the dust of the attic floor. Everything seems to stop. I meet her eyes. She opens her mouth. She begins to say something, begins to reach for me, but the sound is cut off as she crumbles into dust and vanishes, just like the doll.

I don't know how long I sit there, staring at the place my wife used to be – at the dust. My mind is blank. I should cry, I know I should, but my eyes remain dry. All I can think is that she's gone. Gone, and it's my fault.

In time I descended the ladder. The dollhouse is

covered again, the tiny door locked. The brass key goes back on its keyring, the keyring on the hook.

In the morning I call Karina's job, offer explanations. Lies. I think they believe it, but I can't be sure. I think of burning the place down. Burning the dollhouse. But I don't. My doll is still in there and I can't be certain it won't burn even if I leave. I call the real estate agent who sold us the house instead and explain the place needs to go back on the market. She doesn't seem surprised and says she'll get the paperwork started. I gather my belongings – gather Karina's. I take our wedding photo from the mantlepiece and stare blankly at her smiling face. It goes in the same box it was unpacked from just days ago. It will never come back out.

Mango and I leave the house that same day. As I load the car up I catch sight of the neighbours watching me. I stare at them, dead-eyed, and they stare back. Then they shake their heads sadly and go back inside. They know, I'm suddenly sure of it.

As I put the car in gear and pull out I glance back at the house, just once. It was supposed to be our forever home; we had such plans, Karina and I. Then I turn a corner and it vanishes from sight, but I know that up there, in the attic, waiting for the next owner, stands the dollhouse.

DYLAN THOMAS EXPERIENCES ENIGMATIC VISITATIONS IN HIS BOATHOUSE

MARGARET ROYALL

The great man said, on discovering the boathouse at Laugharne:

'... a black-magical bedlam by the sea ... timeless, beautiful, barmy... there is nowhere like it anywhere on earth'

She comes to him nightly, a traveller in time,
with moon-dust braiding her tumbling curls.

Flying through the window at first hint of dusk
she gentles into his dreams, aura bright as
      peacock pomp,

taunting him, transfixing his gaze, her jewel eyes
lucent with desert-dropped stars of biblical myth.

She brushes his cheeks with her feathered wings,
baptises him with salt tears from ancient sea caves,

calling up memories of cool glacial streams,
where ancestors once slaked insatiable thirst.

Floating on waves of euphoria they sail in
        bottomless boats,
trawling forgiveness for sins as yet uncommitted,

straining their eyes to recapture the image of
        a paradise
they have only glimpsed in dream-time limbo.

Bathed in the limpid pools of her eyes,
his limbs shake loose the folds of his tattered gown.

He melts into the bliss of her lightness,
        into her honest embrace,
his body trembling, an earthquake at her
        fingertip touch.

Yet at first hint of dawn she vanishes,
        this alluring apparition …
but still her penumbra taunts his mind
        with insatiable desire.

CHRISTMAS IN TIME

DEREK. H. SKINNER

*An angel of the Lord appeared in a dream to
Joseph and said, Herod will be looking for the
child in order to kill him. Take the child and
his mother and escape to Egypt*

A few years after the death of Einstein, his ideas on
time travel received a brief reawakening when a
few milliseconds were shaved off a speeding timepiece
compared with an identical static companion. This was
proof indeed that the speeding timepiece had actually
travelled a few milliseconds back in time. However,
Einstein's further calculation that it would be necessary
to travel at the speed of light to achieve any significant
forays into the past, effectively placed the kybosh on
the practicality of time travel, leaving it only to be aired
in the realms of science fiction.

It was the discovery of a method to transmogrify
both organic and inorganic matter into nanoparticles,
which suddenly made time travel feasible. When placed
in a magnetron accelerator, these nanoparticles could
achieve speeds in excess of light. Also they always revert
back to their original state once acceleration ceases,
thus making it physically possible for both individuals
and support mechanisms to travel into the past.

This spawned an immediate bonanza for teams of international lawyers and legislators spewing out a plethora of international laws and regulations on time travel, much as it had when AI had first been developed.

The media, of course, went wild. Much of history had to be rewritten and rethought. Videos eavesdropping on conversations with past greats were now possible.

Eminent physicists of course claimed the credit for this breakthrough, but the real instigator and the genius behind it all received no recognition.

Trevor Witherington Spenser, truly worthy to follow in Einstein's footsteps, was a devoutly religious man. Largely indifferent to public acclaim, he disapproved of all the brouhaha his discovery had generated. Working from the Institute for Scientific Research, now better known by the name of the illustrious family on whose estate at the heart of Cirencester it now stands, his desire was only to bring truth and enlightenment to his fellow man.

It was the sudden death of Joy, Spenser's beloved wife, from bowel cancer that was to change not only history, but the future as well. Theirs had been a strange romance. Both had felt an instant recognition the moment they met, as if their union was somehow ordained by heaven. Both knew they were destined for each other. It made their parting so much harder now.

Following his discovery, Spenser's extraordinary mind had wrestled with another tantalising challenge. If one could travel into the past by speeding up nano cells he reasoned, why could not one travel into the future by slowing them down. It wasn't long before he devised a way of doing so.

By this means, he would be able to bring back cures from the future for all diseases, sparing millions from the agonies of suffering and bereavement that he was enduring. Doubtless too it would allow science and technology with one giant bound to leap the centuries. What a tribute that would be to Joy's memory!

Spencer's laboratory now became his solace and his escape from grief. Undisturbed and alone in his laboratory in Cirencester one Christmas day he prepared in secret for his departure. There were dangers. Nano cells decay as they move through time, initially at a rate which the body can regenerate, but thereafter decay accelerates exponentially, and there is no recovery. Effectively, this limited time travel to within a millennium of the origin point.

He started the Magnetron. At once the historic town of Cirencester appeared briefly below him with all its familiar landmarks, bathed in Christmas lights. He could see the German fair which returned every Christmas to the Market Place, the old Abbey Church, now the Parish Church and as he seemed to rise above the town the outline of the old walled town became clearly visible. The image became hazy, then turned into a blur as he raced through the decades. Slowly the details began to become distinct and hardened as he reached his destination. Christmas Day two centuries into the future.

Cirencester? Could this really be Cirencester two

hundred years in the future? Yet it must be, He hadn't moved his location. But then gradually he began to recognize some familiar features. The outline of the Bathhurst estate was clearly to be seen now covered in housing developments, the Institute for Scientific Research where he worked was still there and the Market Place, no German Fair though. But something was missing? Of course! There was no Parish Church. In its place was a building which looked more like a Roman Temple than anything else with some sort of hideous statue in the place of honour outside the entrance. But the building itself didn't look modern, rather it looked as if it had been there for a thousand years or more. But that was impossible.

Then it struck him. There were no churches anywhere. There were temple-like buildings, some with elaborate carvings and figures, but definitely no churches to be seen.

How could it have changed so much? He had dialled in exactly two hundred years. But here there was no evidence of Christmas Day either, no Christmas Trees, no municipal decorations, no signs of Christmas on people's houses. In this century it seemed as if Christianity itself did not exist, as if it had been expunged from human memory.

To Spenser his duty was clear.

Already his Nano-cell Indicator was dangerously low. This was his moment of destiny. He reversed the magnetron to the very first Christmas Day.

He could see the star, like another moon hanging

over one spot. Something else too. In the tiny village just before the small town of Bethlehem were Herod's soldiers. They had surrounded the village. With horror he watched them dragging babies from their mother's arms and slaughtering them. Mothers too, crazed by what they saw, were being indiscriminately slain. But the soldiers were not having it all their own way. Groups of young men had gathered armed with clubs, some with swords or agricultural implements as weapons. There were shepherds, some only children armed with slings, the traditional weapon of their trade. But elsewhere, by sheer weight of arms and discipline the soldiers were prevailing. There was no time to lose.

The stable was not difficult to find bathed in the light of the star. As he neared the place, Spenser reflected upon the scenes he had just witnessed which seemed out of accord with the accounts passed down. Was this the fault in time at work? Or was it simply that the story was over two thousand years old and had been the work of a multitude of writers, all with different points of view, told and retold countless thousands of times? Now would be the crucial test.

Spenser entered the stable. As he stood there a man stepped forward urging him to be quiet for the babe slept. For a moment he gazed in awe. He was in a stable right enough he reflected, but other than the donkey there were no other creatures there. Instead, the place was filled with wine casks, old bed frames, furniture and all the detritus of the innkeeper's trade. It was a mile away from all the cosy images of his childhood.

But time was running out. They didn't seem to realise their danger. And he was feeling weaker already.

A donkey stood quietly chewing hay beside where the baby lay. Using the side of the donkey as a makeshift screen he replayed from his communicator the scenes he had just witnesses to an astonished Joseph. Using the translator, he spoke to Joseph, "Herod will be looking for the child in order to kill him. Take the child and his mother to Egypt …"

Joseph, distraught, needed no second bidding. He roused his wife and began to load the donkey with their frugal possessions amongst which were a few items, expensively wrapped, from which emanated a sharp pungent aroma more familiar to the most expensive of funerals. Spenser also caught the dull gleam of gold. So that part of the Christmas myth held true, he thought. At least it would fund their stay in Egypt.

Now too weak to stand, he waved aside Joseph's offer of help, urging him to leave. At the last moment the mother, cradling her sleeping babe, turned to thank him. To gaze upon the sleeping child was for Spenser the supreme moment of his life. The lines of the Nunc Dimittis sprang into his mind, "Lord now letest thy servant depart in peace, for mine eyes have seen thy salvation."

He was alone, sustained only by that joyous strength that was to fill the souls of martyrs and saints of the future. Soon now, he would be united once again with his own beloved Joy in a realm where time as we understand it has no significance. Truly, their marriage in the future would indeed be a marriage made in heaven. He understood it all. What a blessing there were no children to grieve for them in a different time.

His peaceful thoughts were shattered as the soldiers burst in having been told of a baby's cries in the manger. The manger was empty. The draught from the open door agitated the little pile of dust that marked the last resting place of Trevor Witherington Spenser. A soldier observed a curious looking metal object that seemed to pulsate and glow. He reached forward to grasp it, but in that instant, it vanished. A trick of the light perhaps, he thought.

Nearly twenty-two centuries would pass before Spenser's story became known when his communicator, equipped with its own homing device returned to its starting point in real time. Only then was Spenser's sacrifice revealed. Boxing Day from that day forward would be celebrated as Saint Spencer's Day, after the very first Christmas martyr.

THE GIFT

DAPHNE DENLEY

Am in the search through dusty loft
In treasures of past and things forgot
Eerie stench in the mouldy and aged
Sundries collected, the once loved saved

Boxes that surprise, remembering stories
Heartfelt tears and days of glory
Bursting inside, as reliving old feelings
When really should be sorting and cleaning

Balancing beams, not stepping on ceilings
Into the eaves and the darkest clearings
Cobwebs and spiders, carcasses of flies
Nests and nasties from bats, rats and mice

Wind whistles the rafters, light bulb flickers
I look behind as this gives me the shivers
Perhaps not alone, is a presence lurking?
So speeding up, the sorting and searching

Into the beyond, light catches my eyes
Something sparkling, I turn in surprise
Holding breath, I stare crouched and still
Then crawl towards, intrigued and thrilled

Light was reflection, of a shiny gold clasp
On a light purple box with a fluffy white cat
My first jewellery box that gran had bought
Remember selecting with her in the shop

Excitement again, like the first time I held
Opened the lid and its magic expelled
Ballerina danced to music of swan lake
In front of a mirror with pink felt lined case

In that instant, in a flicker of my eyes
Transported back now by my gran's side
I look around the room, it's Christmas time!
Together my family and all still alive

Happiest times, carefree innocent child
Worries a few and just loving my life
Everyone joyful, been together all day
Crackers, cuddles and loving to play

Passing the parcel and ring on the string
Oranges, chocolates, sugary minced things
Party hats, laughter, songs and good vibes
Keeping awake until worn out and tired

Suddenly the music of swan lake is back
Lying on the attic floor, staring into black
Slowly the feelings and smells disappear
Vision so vivid, hard believe am back here

I rewind the key on the back of the box
Closing the lid, then holding it near
The magic of life truly still carries on
As in what we treasure, memories belong

A jewellery box gift or a vortex to the past
Hoping dreams so real will always last
Forever keep this box, and secrets of mine
Will open again, time after time, after time

PANTOUM

THE ASPIRATIONS OF ANGELS

JULIE WILTSHIRE

I stroll amongst the brooding darkness,
    mantled by a mystical mist.
Upon the ethereal skies, my approaching end
    is scripted.
As my epitaph is scrawled in fairy dust amongst
    the sinking of the day,
The moon slowly rises above the Severn and shines
    its magical light.

Upon the ethereal skies, my approaching end
    is scripted.
This life's fairy-tale, has it a happy ending?
The moon slowly rises above the Severn and shines
    its magical light,
As I tremble along the ragged edges of my
    disappearing world.

This life's fairy-tale, has it a happy ending?
Did I achieve the aspirations of angels?
As I tremble along the ragged edge of my
      disappearing world,
I hear the sweetest notes of compassion played
      upon a flute.

Did I achieve the aspirations of angels?
I stroll amongst the brooding darkness,
      mantled by a mystical mist.
I hear the sweetest notes of compassion played
      upon a flute,
As my epitaph is scrawled in fairy dust,
      amongst the sinking of the day.

NELLIE'S CANDLE

TOBY CRABBE

Autumn arrived. With it, Nellie Jones had taken to dallying about her way home from school, if for nothing more than an opportunity to meander through the neatly sparse woodlands; ambling along the dappled paths looping Hillbury Heath, themselves heavily padded by hardwood and unripe bramble patches. She revelled in discovering the seasonal redness of the local wildlife: the squirrels, the foxes; goldfinches, passing away the golden hours by spying them in the indistinct undergrowth and sketching their image in her own personal journal.

The book was leather-bound and chestnut brown, threadbare and crowded with the many stained trappings of worn parchment that had since bulked out the binding far beyond sensibility or efficiency. Nellie bore no astounding capability; the drawings were merely sharp and feathered facsimiles of the original subjects, with only the most prominent features of their rough anatomy jumping from the page in esprit scruffiness, and yet not one day went by without a new drawing and novel obsession.

One night, when Nellie first caught herself by candlelight, she had expected to view herself in the likeness of something similarly fascinating.

What that moniker meant and denoted to her was uncertain; cryptic. Nevertheless, she periodically pondered the notion of appearing herself in a framed painting. Ordinarily reminded by her warm, dowager grandmother: Agnes (an amiable cobbler and Nellie's minder), that her name bore rosy promise in a manner comparable to the luminance of a midsummer's sun, Nellie dreamed up a doppelganger in a menagerie of hanging portraits. She envisioned her tumbling locks of polished, spiced ginger and her own hazel, gold-flecked eyes brushed amongst delusions of grandeur and gilded luxury. Perhaps an enigmatic and peculiar dignitary, fine dining in a deluxe manor hall or gallery, her countenance emphasised and complimented by the cosy brightness of the hearth, the upstanding sconces; the flambeaus.

Nellie was wrong and had unknowingly been deceiving herself with possibilities, falsifying an untruth and misrepresenting what she came to see as she gripped the candle at a bedside mirror. Nellie's bedroom chamber was dainty and collected puddles of shadow, drawing back all semblance of softness from her pale features and carrying them away into the late-evening darkness. Only a sallow caricature of angular, macabre expression gazed back in reflection, her drippy candle bawling into a burnished, bronze basin. Neither abject beauty nor gooey-eyed appeal could be distinguished. The light only dimly illuminating her sharp brow and rounded chin, the shade delicately peeled away the ingredients of her full mask, with naught but a ghoulish approximation of the child's aspect remaining in place.

Nellie leaned in with an inquisitive glower, absorbed by how the mirror distorted her image like the surface of a still-wet, oily canvas, before recoiling at the creamy bite of paraffin wax running down her fingers. She spiralled back, her motion briskly extinguishing the wick and dropping the holder to the floorboards with a blunder. The basin continued rolling, tinny and loud prior to the undulation slowing to a gentle, conspicuous halt.

Before the child had buried herself beneath blanket and quilted herself in a self-imposed blackness, she had been met with an aged holler from the workshop below. The voice was deadened by dark wood, albeit identifiably enveloping, bearing a baked disparity of honeyed warmth and a bootstrap, leathery harshness.

Agnes, 'Nana', inquired as to the origin of the cumbersome bluster from above, whether or not any harm had been done to the child and her valuable mementos and as to why her granddaughter was not dozing deeply during an hour as dusky as this.

Peeking outwards through her ocular window, barely ajar and letting slip wisps of seasonal breeze, Nellie beheld the quaint residences planted downside the hillock's promenade.

In their numbers, they formed bowed, cambered lanes of cobbled complexion, narrow passageways of burnt brick and rusty, leafed canopies. Shrouded by an eve of obscurity, the bewitching hour came to pass high above the antiquated boulevard, where Nellie peered through her bundled duvet to find them once again, to prove to herself she was not muddled by another sleepless daze.

Nebulous and silent in baroque monotony, a sea of milky candles was spawning in the black. She could see them again, they were real. Much like the nights before, dancing wick-spirits – 'Humours', Nana called them in her old bedtime convictions – had begun whispering into fiery matter and lively zeal behind numerous open-balcony doors far across Hillbury Heath and beyond.

They were nothing if not beautiful.

Nellie watched them flicker, feathery and slight, waltzing and chanting about the heavy-headed crowns of men, women and children, as campers were to do about their encampment in song. Not once did she remove her eyes from the fantastical absurdity of their existence, until she allowed a heavy, pensive dreaminess to begin its murmuring.

Only then would she allow herself to numb and fade into a pleasantly bemused slumber.

And candle warmth drew in around her.

A SPOOKY MISUNDERSTANDING

MARGARET ROYALL

Dear Reader,

I'm letting you into a secret as yet untold; a scary event in my teenage years that terrified me.

One dark, windy November evening my parents had to leave me alone in our bungalow for the first time ever. I was a teenager, fifteen years old and according to law I could be left alone, no problem there. However, I was not a confident teenager in some respects. As an only child my parents had always been very protective of me, you could say over-protective, especially if I needed to go out on cold, dark winter evenings. One parent would always accompany me to my music lesson, youth club or wherever and walk me home again. If the weather was really bad my father would drive me to the venue in our old Austin 7 car.

On the evening in question storm clouds were gathering in the sky and the light breeze of earlier in the day was becoming a gale, although it was still light when they left and I felt confident. My Nanna had suffered a stroke and was recuperating in her home on the far side of town. As my mum was her only daughter it fell to her to care for Nanna whenever she could. Mostly this was in the daytime when I was at school. In the evenings Nanna's younger sister, who lived close by, would take over. On this occasion, however, there had been an urgent telephone call, informing my mum that Nanna had taken a turn for the worse and summoning her to go round. Dad offered to drive her there to save walking the two miles, but Mum was worried about leaving me alone.

'You're sure you'll be ok?' she said. 'I can ask a neighbour to sit with you if you like?'

'Of course I will. Don't fret about me. I've homework to do for my Maths O level. I'll lock the doors after you,' I said.

Adrenalin coursed through my veins as I locked up and sat down to tackle the hated Maths homework. I was actually delighted to be trusted enough to be left alone. Of course, I'd been left in the daytime for short periods while Mum went to Townswomen's Guild or round to visit a sick friend or to the corner shop, but never at night. I glanced out of the window at the darkening sky. Shadows were starting to fall across the garden. The two upright posts of the swing were casting long shadows onto the lawn. I shuddered, noticing that they looked like a gallows in the half light. Quickly I closed the curtains, switched on the kitchen and living room lights and shut the connecting door. Back to the hated Maths. In 1959 we didn't own a TV set, so there was no possibility of switching that on as a distraction.

Besides, I was forbidden to play the radio or listen to my pop records on my Dansette record player until all homework had been done. Silence reigned, apart from the sound of the wind rattling furiously at the window frames. It penetrated the gaps between frame and pane and made the flimsy cotton curtains billow out in a ghostly manner. I shuddered but told myself not to be stupid.

I dutifully completed the Maths homework, but just as I was packing my books back into my satchel, I heard a sudden, strange sound, a swoosh, coming from down the hallway. I froze to the spot, ears pricked, listening for further sounds. There it was again, swoosh, and a muffled bang. I sprang to my feet, the hairs on the back of my neck standing up. Was there someone in the house? A burglar? For a moment I was rooted to the spot, then my courage deserted me and the flight or fight instinct kicked in. Grabbing my school gabardine from the hook by the back door, I hurtled out through the gate, down the side alley and onto Sherburn Street. I ran and ran, as fast as my legs would go, right through town, heading towards my former primary school. My Nanna's house stood opposite. I banged on the front door like a maniac and burst into floods of tears as Dad opened it.

'What on earth's happened?' he said, taking me in his arms and cuddling me tight.

'Someone … in the house … a ghostly sound … an intruder …' I gasped, clinging to my dad like a limpet.

He sat me down in the kitchen, poured me a glass of

water and once he'd managed to calm me down a little I explained what had happened. Dad was puzzled but remained calm, not wanting to show his concern and alarm me further.

'I'm sure there's a very reasonable explanation for it,' he said. 'Come on, we'll drive home and take a look. Don't be scared, I'm here with you. It'll be nothing to worry about, you'll see.'

We drove home, parked up and entered the property. I had neglected to lock the back door in my haste and the living room light was still burning. Purposefully, Dad switched on all the lights and strode down the hallway making plenty of noise. He inspected each of the bedrooms in turn. Suddenly he burst into gales of laughter.

'Come and look. I think I've found the culprit,' he said.

Nervously I joined him in my parents' bedroom. He pointed to two shirts on hangers that were lying in a crumpled heap on the floor.

'Look, I left these shirts hanging from the picture rail.' He turned and pointed to the bedroom window that was about 4 inches ajar. 'The wind has got up this evening. A gust of wind must have caught them and caused them to topple. You heard the swoosh of the fabric against the wall, then the bang as the hangers crashed against the skirting board.' He smiled reassuringly.

I felt a huge sense of relief but then immediately acute embarrassment. How could I have been so stupid?

I should have had the courage to go and investigate. I would have soon realised what had occurred.

'I'm sorry I was such a coward,' I said. 'I should have known it was unlikely to be a burglar.'

Dad patted my shoulder. 'No need to apologise. You couldn't have known. Now, all's well. Let's go pick your mum up. She needs to know we're safe,' he said, then whispered in my ear. 'Your secret ghost story is safe with me. I won't tell if you don't!'

And I never have told anyone … until today. And now, you must promise me you will keep the secret too!

THE DAY OUT

DAPHNE DENLEY

I'm very excited as a mystery day out
In the car travelling – no idea whereabouts
Days away in the past have been just a few
The park, pool, seaside and the zoo
I really am happy, anticipation balloons
They've kept this quiet, so must be good
Signpost they tease, 'are we nearly there?'
Arrive at a theme park with a huge funfair
Now scream with delight, as just realised
The chance to go on the daring thrill rides
Often I've dreamt of and tried to imagine
Never knew one day that it would happen
Turning out much better than I thought
On rollercoasters dive, twist, turn and jolt
Running between the next experience
Each as daring, but thrills a bit different
Time for a break, fast food a plenty
Chips, burger, donut and pop filled belly
Off for the next round of fun to be had
New area in the theme park, 'what is that?'
Dart off alone towards the big rides ahead
Huge loops impress, look fast and the best
Can't wait any longer so I join a queue
Look only forward at ride high in the blue

Sitting next to a stranger, as excited as me
It's their first time too, wonder how it'll be
Smile at each other hold tight and sit back
Screaming and laughter as going so fast
Finished, still buzzing, catching my breath
Look back at the exit, I have no regrets
Must find my parents, are surely behind
Scan all directions, but may need to go find
I wait for a while, in case they got on later
As I ran on in front, as I was far too eager
Something isn't right, stop in confusion
No parents in sight, but only other children
Panicking frantically I now search around
Straight past the rides, newly had found
Children around me don't seem to care
Hypnotised trance, just run around the fair
Early evening darkness starts to descend
Aimlessly walking to find parents I depend
Tears start to fall as giving up on it all
Out of the mist I hear a loud call
'Wake up, wake up' I'd fallen asleep
'We've arrived at the fair, look can you see'
Baffled but happy to do all over again
Get out of the car and day out begin
Enjoying my day, but wary this time
Not running off leaving my parents behind
See familiar faces, is this deja vu?
Or still asleep and this nightmare is true?

MIDDAY MOON

OLIVE MALCOLM

Lying in wait
winter's icy sepulchre
claims her victims

A frozen track leads far into the forest,
the ancient realm of hunter and hunted,
where bear lurks and wolf prowls
and the mighty elk roams free.

In midwinter twilight, when the sun hides
and moon reigns, the Ice Maiden
weaves mystic incantations, luring
intrepid huntsmen into her Arctic bondage.

They leave blood offerings to appease
the forest gods and follow her lilting voice
ever deeper into the wilderness, engulfed
by tangled branches laden with snow.

Enchanted by the maiden's soft lament,
they lose all sense of time or place
as, one by one, they fall asleep –
the frozen earth their pillow and their grave.

A pentangle of sound touches the icebound land
as warmth flows from the kantele's silver strings,
conjuring up the sleeping sun and calling
migrating birds to journey north again.

The Ice Maiden's time is past,
her flaxen hair melts like drifts of snow,
bone-white flesh fades, transformed
into the faint shadow of a tree   waiting.

Inspired by the Kalevala, a 19th century
collection of Finnish legend and folklore.

Midday Moon refers to the darkest time
of year when the Land of the Midnight
Sun is shrouded in darkness and daylight
hours are scarce.

The kantele is a traditional five-stringed
musical instrument made of birch wood.

A RECONCILIATION OF TROLLS

STEPHEN CONNOLLY

He wakes with the first knock. (Thump) And curses. After all these years, why can't he remember to put it in the calendar?

Stumbling downstairs, (Thump) feet cold on the kitchen tiles, (THUMP) scrabbling for the back door key, (THUMP!) the chill air reminding him of his dressing gown hanging on the bathroom door.

They glare at him, the band of Trolls waiting in his back garden, lined up along the path. He'd never wanted a path, but after years of their vast feet obliterating the grass, he'd given in and had one laid. A final acceptance of the situation, but the last straw for his wife. She'd packed a bag and left the same day. He couldn't blame her.

The Trolls are ... *immense*. Even the youngster – he can't quite make himself think *runt* – towers over him. As always, they make no attempt at a greeting or even to acknowledge his presence. Their faces show only the same, sullen resentment: *Why are you still here?*

One by one, they stoop and squeeze into his kitchen, forcing him back. It's almost comic, watching them struggle. Are they entering his house, or putting it on, like a tight suit? Either way, he retreats quickly. A fall would be almost certainly fatal, for they would not think to stop or go around. And no health insurance company will touch him.

Their first appearance had been terrifying. He and his wife, barely a month in their smart new home, fast asleep on a Sunday morning ... awoken by the menacing THUMP at the back door. He'd had no idea Trolls migrated – even now, Troll studies are not compulsory on the curricula of our city's schools. And the Trolls themselves have never been any help, unwilling or unable to explain their presence, the primal urge to follow an ancestral pathway that just happens to bisect his home. In autumn, south. In spring, back north.

The police had not been sympathetic: 'So? Just let them through!'

'I *told* you this place was too cheap!' his wife had said. 'But Oh No! You knew *better*.' All too late he remembered the estate agent's vague reference to 'migration'. Birds, he'd assumed.

They had barely gone back to bed when the next troop had arrived and they had the entire experience to live through again. In the end, it had taken the best part of a week for the entire tribe(?) to pass, arriving in groups large and small, at all hours of the day and night. He didn't think to keep a tally, but it would have easily run well into the hundreds.

Their marriage had struggled from then on in. One transit was bad enough, but the idea of dealing with them twice yearly, for the rest of their lives in the house? That's when she began forgetting her keys, an unconscious rejection of the house.

They'd sued the vendor, of course. Also the estate agent, the solicitor, the planning department … anybody with the vaguest connection to the house. But to no avail. In our city, regular courts have no jurisdiction over Trolls, only a single specialist court, sitting infrequently, their backlog of cases stretching for years. He's been waiting for news of a judgement, even compensation, for almost a decade, but there has been no progress. And who will buy the place now?

The Trolls squeeze into the hall, long emptied of breakables, shaking the house around them. So much had been destroyed during that first, nightmare transit. Photographs, ornaments, knickknacks. He grits his teeth, listening to the unmistakeable sounds of a slate slowly sliding down the roof to immolate itself on the front path.

Too late, he remembers the front door is still shut, with Trolls between him and it. With no alternative he … *squeezes* his way between them – like some surreal version of swimming – their coarse woollen clothing scratching his face, their mottled, meaty hands swinging close to his head, their pungent Troll smell thick in his nostrils. Fortunately, the door now opens outwards or they might all be stuck inside for the day. That first time had been a nightmare experience, the urgent calls to the Fire Brigade, ignored for hours.

With time, he'd imagined them becoming … friendlier? Nodding when they arrived, perhaps? But they're Trolls. As unfathomable and unpleasant now as at their first appearance. Each transit proved unique, numbers and groupings constantly varying, meaning that there was never any way to gauge how far along in the process you might be on any particular day.

Where do they go? His wife had been occasionally curious. What do they do there? Moving so slowly, surely by the time they arrive it must be time to turn round and come home? Once a transit had begin, no other topics could be discussed, or held any interest.

For a while, after a Transit things seemed to get back to normal. They persevered, made the best of things, but his original failure always felt too close to the surface, a constant presence lurking behind every argument, unable to be forgotten or forgiven. She couldn't help blaming him, and he couldn't blame her for it.

With a final squirm he reaches the front door. He opens it and the Trolls begin exiting, one by one, without a backward glance, heading for the next house between them and wherever they will spend winter.

Over the years he's tried everything to repel, redirect or even somehow … *educate* them. Barbed wire front and back, placards detailing the law of trespass, signage indicating alternate routes … until the neighbours threatened lawsuits, fearing visits of their own. He'd considered sirens, to alert those downstream, or a campaign for public networks of observers. But why should he go to the trouble and expense? Nobody's ever bothered to alert *him*.

He closes the front door, the house feeling strangely

empty. He bends to examine the object one of them has deposited by the stairs. A tradition perhaps? Or their idea of a Toll? *Something for your inconvenience.* In the past, they've left pages from books, half-eaten sandwiches, even a thigh bone. Human, according to the police. This time … a car tyre. It's too random to be irritating.

He leans against the wall and considers. It's not worth going back to bed, the next … squad will already be drawing near. Not for the first time he wishes they'd all travel *together*. It would be worth losing a day or two, just to know it was over for the season.

He misses his wife. They'd had such plans. To travel, have children, build a life together in their dream home. Any bitterness he felt at her parting has long gone. He hopes she's found happiness somewhere, that she sometimes spares him a thought, even. In the spring, or autumn, does she ever feel a pang, remembering him and the good times they had? Does she ever sympathise with what he will shortly be going through?

Technically they're still married, no divorce paperwork ever having arrived. But this is when he misses her most, in the wake of a transit.

He should do the rounds, check for items needing bracing, note down the numbers for his records – his insurance company are very specific. But for the first time the situation seems so ridiculous, all he can do is laugh. Uncaring of how it might seem to another, he just leans against the wall, shoulders shaking with simple, honest laughter.

Which is why he doesn't hear it at first, yet more noise from the kitchen: Tap, tap, *tap*.

The sound so familiar, so delicate compared to the *THUMPING* of Trolls. The memory so keen: *she was forever forgetting her keys.* He can't move at first, terrified of breaking the spell. But it's a matter of seconds, his return to the back door. The shortest of journeys.